The King of Pirates

The King of Pirates

Daniel Defoe

ET REMOTISSIMA PROPE

100 PAGES

100 PAGES

Published by Hesperus Press Limited
4 Rickett Street, London SW6 1RU
www.hesperuspress.com

First published by Hesperus Press Limited, 2002

Foreword © Peter Acrkoyd, 2002

Designed and typeset by Fraser Muggeridge
Printed in the United Arab Emirates by Oriental Press

ISBN: 1-84391-011-X

CONTENTS

FOREWORD

The King of Pirates was written in 1719, immediately after the success of *Robinson Crusoe*, and was directly dependent upon it for its formula both of sea adventure and of fantasy masquerading as fact. It was published anonymously by its author, Daniel Defoe, just as *The Life and Strange Surprising Adventures of Robinson Crusoe* was advertised as 'by Himself', as if to vouchsafe its honesty and reliability as a work of documentation rather than of fanciful literature. The hero of this adventure, Captain Avery, was subsequently used by Defoe in another bestseller; it is the rule of great popular novelists never to let a sensational character die.

By sleight of hand Defoe commends his fabricated if magnificent story as an antidote to all 'former ridiculous and extravagant accounts' of Avery and his piratical crew. Throughout his long and immensely prolific career, in fact, Defoe was constantly dressing up the works of his imagination as 'true' and 'faithful' reports. His *Journal of the Plague Year* was invented some fifty-seven years after the events it purports to describe, and his *Tour through the Whole Island of Great Britain* was written from his house in Stoke Newington.

In fact Defoe had begun as a journalist before he ever turned to fiction, and it is doubtful whether he saw any difference between the two activities. He invented what might be termed the poetry of fact, and *The King of Pirates*, for example, is filled with minute particulars and circumstantial detail; the reality of the landscapes and seascapes is emphasised in order to lend authenticity to the dramatic stories that unfold upon them. Narratives of the sea have in any case always held a special fascination for English readers, ever since the publication of Hakluyt's *Voyages*, and Defoe had an instinctive grasp of public taste. There was hardly a contemporaneous marvel or an adventure that he did not graphically describe in poem, pamphlet or book. The detail is indeed so specific that it commands assent in even the most distrustful reader. His language here is exact as well as colourful, with a cadence not unlike that of rapid colloquial speech; the power comes from the inflections of an apparently single and honest voice. Thus we seem to be listening to the true demotic of the eighteenth century – 'These big words amazed the fellows, and answered my end to a tittle; for they told such rodomontading stories of us…'

It is often a matter of debate whether Defoe's casual and colloquial style was the result of accident or of design. Was it deliberately achieved, or was it the consequence of rapid and careless composition? It seems likely, however, that it was indeed the product of conscious artistry. He was inventing an appropriate voice for Captain Avery with no less skill than that with which he invented the 'facts' of his notorious career. As a result Avery's narrative is filled with humour and with drama. When a Catholic friar begs that his silver plate be returned, because they are consecrated to the Virgin, Avery remarks that 'as it happened, he could not persuade us to it'. There speaks the ironical Protestant.

The life of Defoe itself was both strange and surprising; he was a paid spy, an agent provocateur, a bankrupt and sometime inmate of Newgate prison who was forced to stand in the pillory. This is perhaps the reason for his close identification with the pirate king himself, a man who must survive by his wits upon the sea of life and whose morality is – to say the least – ambiguous. He admits to his own frailties very readily – 'This innocent usage began to rouse some good nature in me (though I never had much)'. Defoe was always able to write convincingly about the plight and conduct of the 'outsider', just as he was able to depict the solitariness of Robinson Crusoe. It has been suggested in turn that Crusoe is the type or epitome of economic man, and in the career of Captain Avery we might also find some caricature or symbol of the commercial avarice of the typical eighteenth-century Londoner. That is why Defoe was happy to enumerate all the profits and merchandise of Avery's various expeditions – 'the value of 16,000 pieces of eight in gold of Chile, as good as any in the world' – in order to satisfy the native appetite for trade and commerce of every description. The world of *The King of Pirates* is a desperate one, of essentially rapacious individuals who consort with each other only for gain and who can only be curbed by violence. It is the world of Hobbes' *Leviathan* transported to the high seas.

It is also a tract for the burgeoning new empire being created by Defoe's contemporaries, and Avery's sojourn in Madagascar may be seen as a picture in miniature of the English appropriation and exploitation of North America and India. *The King of Pirates* is a tale of acquisitiveness in which a nation, as well as an individual, is the true subject. This is perhaps made more explicit by Defoe in one of the most cogent and arresting passages of the narrative: 'I told them the Romans themselves were, at first, no better than such a gang of rovers as we were, and who knew but our General, Captain Avery might lay the foundation of as great an empire as they.'

Yet this is no tract or polemic but, rather, an intensely dramatic narrative in which action and sensation are the defining elements. If Defoe can claim the palm as the first of the English novelists, then *The King of Pirates* can be confirmed as one of the very earliest 'adventure novels' in the language. It closes as suddenly and as peremptorily as it begins; there is no structure in the conventional literary sense and no aspirations towards form. It is simply an episode snatched from circumambient life, a sudden picture of eighteenth-century characters and attitudes – in short, a vision of a lost world.

– *Peter Ackroyd, 2002*

The King of Pirates

The King of Pirates,
Being an Account of the
Famous Enterprises
of Captain Avery*,
the Mock King of
Madagascar,

with

his rambles and piracies,
wherein all the sham accounts
formerly published of him are detected.

In two letters from himself:
one during his stay at Madagascar,
and one since his escape from thence.

---

* Captain Henry Every (1653–96), alias Captain Bridgeman and Long Ben, was also the model for Defoe's *Captain Singleton* (1720).

PREFACE

One of the particular advantages of the following letters from Captain Avery is the satisfaction they will give the readers how much they have been imposed upon in the former ridiculous and extravagant accounts which have been put upon the world in what has been published already.

It has been enough to the writers of this man's life, as they call it, that they could put anything together, to make a kind of monstrous unheard-of story, as romantic as the reports that have been spread about of him. And the more those stories appeared monstrous and incredible, the more suitable they seemed to be to what the world would have been made to expect of Captain Avery.

There is always a great difference between what men say of themselves, and what others say for them when they come to write historically of the transactions of their lives.

The publisher of these letters recommends this performance to the readers, to make their judgement of the difference between them and the extravagant stories already told, and which is most likely to be genuine. And, as they verily believe these letters to be the best and truest account of Captain Avery's piracies that ever has or ever will come to the knowledge of the world, they recommend them as such, and doubt not but they will answer for themselves in the reading.

The account given of Captain Avery's taking the great Mogul's daughter, ravishing and murdering her, and all the ladies of her retinue, is so differently related here, and so extravagantly related before, that it cannot but be a satisfaction to the most unconcerned reader to find such a horrible piece of villainy, as the other was supposed to be, not to have been committed in the world.

On the contrary, we find here that, except plundering the princess of her jewels and money to a prodigious value – a thing which, falling into the hands of freebooters, everyone that had the misfortune to fall into such hands would expect – that, excepting this, the lady was used with all the decency and humanity, and perhaps with more than ever women, falling among pirates, had found before, especially considering that, by report, she was a most beautiful and agreeable person herself, as were also several of those about her.

The booty taken with her, though infinitely great in itself, yet has been so magnified beyond common sense that it makes all the rest that has been said of those things ridiculous and absurd.

The like absurdity in the former relations of this matter is that of the making an offer of I know not how many million to the late Queen, for Captain Avery's pardon, with a petition to the Queen, and her Majesty's negative answer – all which are as much true as his being master of so many millions of money, which neither he nor his gang never had – and of his being proclaimed King of Madagascar, marrying the Mogul's daughter, and the like. And, by the by, it was but ill laid together of those who published that he first ravished her, then murdered her, and then married her; all which are very remarkable for recommending the thing to those that read it.

If those stories are explained here and duly exposed, and the history of Captain Avery set in a fairer light, the end is answered; and of this the readers are to be the only judges. But this may be said, without any arrogance, that this story, stripped of all the romantic, improbable, and impossible parts of it, looks more like the history of Captain Avery than anything yet published ever has done; and, if it is not proved that the Captain wrote these letters himself, the publisher says none but the Captain himself will ever be able to mend them.

A FIRST LETTER

You may be sure I received with resentment enough the account that a most ridiculous book, entitled *My Life and Adventures*, had been published in England, being fully assured nothing of truth could be contained in such a work. And though it may be true that my extravagant story may be the proper foundation of a romance, yet as no man has a title to publish it better than I have to expose and contradict it, I send you this by one of my particular friends, who having an opportunity of returning into England has promised to convey it faithfully to you, by which, at least, two things shall be made good to the world. First, that they shall be satisfied in the scandalous and unjust manner in which others have already treated me; and it shall give, in the meantime, a larger account of what may at present be fit to be made public of my unhappy though successful adventures.

I shall not trouble my friends with anything of my original and first introduction into the world. I leave it to you to add for yourself what you think proper to be known on that subject. Only this I enjoin you to take notice of, that the account printed of me, with all the particulars of my marriage, my being defrauded, and leaving my family and native country on that account, is a mere fable and a made story, to embellish, as the writer of it perhaps supposed, the rest of his story, or perhaps to fill up the book that it might swell to a magnitude which his barren invention could not supply.

In the present account, I have taken no notice of my birth, infancy, youth, or any of that part which, as it was the most useless part of my years to myself so it is the most useless to anyone that shall read this work to know, being altogether barren of anything remarkable in itself, or instructing to others. It is sufficient to me to let the world know, as above, that the former accounts made public are utterly false, and to begin my account of myself at a period which may be more useful and entertaining.

It may be true that I may represent some particulars of my life in this tract with reserve or enlargement such as may be sufficient to conceal anything in my present circumstance that ought to be concealed and reserved with respect to my own safety, and therefore, if on pretence of justice the busy world should look for me in one part of the world when I am in another, search for my new kingdom in Madagascar, and should not find it, or search for my settlement on one side of the island when it lies on another, they must not take this ill; for self-preservation being the supreme law of nature, all things of this kind must submit to that.

In order then to come immediately to my story, I shall without any circumlocutions give you leave to tell the world that, being bred to sea from a youth, none of those romantic introductions published had any share in my adventures, or were any way the cause of my taking the courses I have since been embarked in. But as in several parts of my wandering life I had seen something of the immense wealth which the buccaneers and other adventurers met with in their scouring about the world for purchase, I had for a long time meditated in my thoughts to get possessed of a good ship for that purpose if I could, and to try my fortune. I had been some years in the Bay of Campeche[1], and though with patience I endured the fatigue of that laborious life, yet it was as visible to others as to myself that I was not formed by nature for a logwood cutter any more than I was for a foremast man, and therefore night and day I applied myself to study how I should dismiss myself from that drudgery, and get to be, first or last, master of a good ship –

which was the utmost of my ambition at that time – resolving, in the meantime, that whenever any such thing should happen, I would try my fortune in the cruising trade, but would be sure not to prey upon my own countrymen.

It was many years after this before I could bring my purposes to pass, and I served first in some of the adventures of Captain Sharp, Captain Sawkins, and others, in their bold adventures in the South Seas (where I got a very good booty), was at the taking of Puno[2] – where we were obliged to leave infinite wealth behind us, for want of being able to bring it away – and, after several adventures in those seas, was among that party who fought their way sword in hand through all the detachments of the Spaniards in the journey overland, across the Isthmus of Darien[3], to the north seas. And when others of our men got away – some one way, some another – I, with twelve more of our men, by help of a piragua, got into the Bay of Campeche, where we fell very honestly to cutting of logwood, not for want but to employ ourselves till we could make off.

Here three of our men died, and we that were left shared their money among us; and having stayed here two years, without seeing any way of escape that I dared to trust to, I at last with two of our men who spoke Spanish perfectly well made a desperate attempt to travel over land to L—, having buried all our money (which was worth 8,000 pieces of eight a man, though most of it in gold) in a pit in the earth which we dug twelve foot deep, and where it would have lain still, for no man knew where to look for it. But we had an opportunity to come at it again some years after.

We travelled along the seashore five days together, the weather exceeding hot, and did not doubt but we should so disguise ourselves as to be taken for Spaniards. But our better fortune provided otherwise for us, for the sixth day of our march we found a canoe lying on the shore with no one in her. We found, however, several things in her, which told us plainly that she belonged to some Englishmen who were on shore. So we resolved to sit down by her and wait. By and by we heard the Englishmen, who were seven in number, and were coming back to their boat having been up the country to an ingenio[4], where they had gotten great quantities of provisions, and were bringing it down to their boat which they had left on the shore (with the help of five Indians off whom they had bought it), not thinking there were any people thereabouts. When they saw us, not knowing who we were, they were just going to fire at us, when I perceiving it, held up a white flag as high as I could reach it, which was in short only a piece of an old linen waistcoat which I had on and pulled off for the occasion. Upon this, however, they forbore firing at us, and when they came nearer to us, they could easily see that we were their own countrymen. They enquired of us what we came there for. We told them we had travelled from Campeche where, being tired with the hardships of our fortune, and not getting any vessel to carry us where we durst go, we were even desperate, and cared not what became of us, so that – had not they come to us thus happily – we should have put ourselves into the hands of the Spaniards rather than have perished where we were.

They took us into their boat, and afterwards carried us on board their ship. When we came there we found they were a worse sort of wanderers than ourselves. For though we had been a kind of pirates, known and declared enemies to the Spaniards, yet it was to them only and to no other – for we never offered to rob any of our other European nations, either Dutch or French, much less English – but now we were listed in the service of the Devil indeed, and like him were at war with all mankind.

However, we not only were obliged to sort with them while with them, but in a little time the novelty of the crime wore off, and we grew hardened to it, like the rest. And in this service I spent four years more of my time.

Our captain in this pirate ship was named Nichols, but we called him Captain Redhand. It seems it was a Scots sailor gave him that name when he was not the head of the crew, because he was so bloody a wretch that he scarce ever was at the taking any prize but he had a hand in some butchery or other.

They were hard put to it for fresh provisions, or they would not have sent thus up into the country a single canoe. And when I came on board they were so straitened that, by my advice, they resolved to go to the isle of Cuba to kill wild beef, of which the south side of the island is so full. Accordingly, we sailed thither directly.

The vessel carried sixteen guns, but was fitted to carry twenty-two, and there was on board 160 stout fellows, as bold and as case-hardened for the work as ever I met with upon any occasion whatever. We victualled in this place for eight months, by our calculation. But our cook, who had the management of the salting and pickling the beef, ordered his matters so that, had he been let alone, he would have starved us all, and poisoned us too. For, as we are obliged to hunt the black cattle in the island sometimes a great while before we can shoot them, it should be observed that the flesh of those that are heated before they are killed is not fit to be pickled or salted up for keeping.

But this man happening to pickle up the beef without regard to this particular distinction, most of the beef so pickled stunk before we left the place, so that we were obliged to throw it all away. The men then said it was impossible to salt any beef in those hot countries so as to preserve it, and would have had us give it over, and have gone to the coast of New England or New York for provisions. But I soon convinced them of the mistake, and by only using the caution, viz. not to salt up any beef of those cattle that had been hunted, we cured 140 barrels of very good beef, and such as lasted us a very great while.

I began to be of some repute among them upon this occasion, and Redhand took me into the cabin with him to consult upon all emergencies, and gave me the name of captain, though I had then no command. By this means I gave him an account of all my adventures in the South Seas, and what a prodigious booty we got there with Captain Goignet, the Frenchman, and with Captain Sharp and others, encouraging him to make an attempt that way, and proposing to him to go away to Brazil, and so round the Straits of Magellan or Cape Horn.

However in this he was more prudent than I, and told me that not only the strength but the force of his ship was too small; not but that he had men enough, as he said very well, but he wanted more guns and a better ship. For indeed the ship we were in was but a weak crazy boat for so long a voyage. So he said he approved my project very well, but that he thought we should try to take some more substantial vessel for the business. And, says he, if we could but take a good stout ship fit to carry thirty guns, and a sloop or brigantine, he would go with all his heart.

This I could not but approve of, so we formed the scheme of the design, and he called all his men together and proposed it to them, and they all approved it with a general consent, and I had the honour of being the contriver of the voyage. From this time we resolved somehow or other to get a better ship under us, and it was not long before an opportunity presented to our mind.

Being now upon the coast of the island of Cuba, we stood away west, coasting the island, and so went away for Florida, where we cruised among the islands, and in the wake of the gulf. But nothing presented a great while. At length we spied a sail, which proved an English homeward-bound ship from Jamaica. We immediately chased her and came up with her. She was a stout ship, and the captain defended her very well, and had she not been a cumbered deep ship being full loaded so that they could scarce come at their guns, we should have had our hands full of her. But when they found what we were, and that being full of men, we were resolved to be on board them, and that we had hoisted the black flag – a signal that we would give them no quarter – they began to sink in their spirits, and soon after cried, 'Quarter!', offering to yield. Redhand would have given them no quarter, but according to his usual practice would have thrown the men all into the sea. But I prevailed with him to give them quarter and good usage too, and so they yielded, and a very rich prize it was, only that we knew not what to do with the cargo.

When we came to consider more seriously the circumstances we were in by taking this ship, and what we should do with her, we found that she was not only deep laden but was a very heavy sailer, and that, in short, she was not such a ship as we wanted. So upon long debate, we resolved to take out of her all the rum, the indigo, and the money we could come at, with about twenty casks of sugar and twelve of her guns, with all the ammunition, small arms, bullets, etc. and let her go, which was accordingly done, to the great joy of the captain that commanded her. However, we took in her about 6,000 pounds sterling in pieces of eight.

But the next prize we met suited us better on all accounts, being a ship from Kinsale in Ireland laden with beef and butter and beer for Barbados. Never was ship more welcome to men in our circumstances. This was the very thing we wanted. We saw the ship early in the morning, at about five leagues' distance, and we were three days in chase of her. She stood from us, as if she would have run away from the Cape Verde Islands, and two or three times we thought she sailed so well she would have got away from us, but we had always the good luck to get sight of her in the morning. She was about 260 tons, an English frigate-built ship, and had twelve guns on board, but could carry twenty. The commander was a Quaker, but yet had he been equal to us in force it appeared by his countenance he would not have been afraid of his flesh, or have baulked using the carnal weapon of offence, viz. the cannon-ball.

We soon made ourselves master of this ship when once we came up with him, and he was everything that we wanted. So we began to shift our guns into her, and shifted about sixty tons of her butter and beef into our own frigate. This made the Irish vessel be a clear ship, lighter in the water, and have more room on board for fight if occasion offered.

When we had the old quaking skipper on board, we asked him whether he would go along with us. He gave us no answer at first, but when we asked him again he returned that he did not know whether it might be safe for him to answer the question. We told him he should either go or stay as he pleased. 'Why then,' says he, 'I had rather ye will give me leave to decline it.'

We gave him leave, and accordingly set him on shore afterwards at Nevis, with ten of his men. The rest went along with us as volunteers, except the carpenter and his mate, and the surgeon – those we took by force. We were now supplied as well as heart could wish, had a large ship in our possession with provisions enough for a little fleet rather than for a single ship. So with this purchase we went away for the Leeward Islands, and fain we would have met with some of the New York or New England ships, which generally come laden with peas, flour, pork, etc. But it was a long while before anything of that kind presented. We had promised the Irish captain to set him on shore with his company at Nevis, but we were not willing till we had done our business in those seas, because of giving the alarm among those islands. So we went away for St Domingo[5], and making that island our rendezvous, we cruised to the eastward in hopes of some purchase. It was not long before we spied a sail, which proved to be a Bermuda sloop, but bound from Virginia or Maryland with flour, tobacco and some malt, the last a thing which in particular we knew not what to do with. However, the flour and tobacco were very welcome, and the sloop no less welcome than the rest, for she was a very large vessel and carried near sixty tons, and when not so deep laden, proved an excellent sailer. Soon after this we met with another sloop, but she was bound from Barbados to New England, with rum, sugar, and molasses. Nothing disturbed us in taking this vessel, but that being willing enough to let her go (for as to the sugar and molasses, we had neither use for them, or room for them), but to have let her go had been to give the alarm to all the coast of North America, and then what we wanted would never come in our way. Our Captain, justly called Redhand or Bloodyhand, was presently for dispatching them that they might tell no tales. And indeed the necessity of the method had very near prevailed. Nor did I much interpose here, I know not why. But some of the other men put him in as good a way, and that was to bring the sloop to an anchor under the lee of St Domingo, and take away all her sails that she should not stir till we gave her leave.

We met with no less than five prizes more here in about twenty days' cruise, but none of them for our turn; one of them, indeed, was a vessel bound to St Christopher[6] with Madeira wine. We borrowed about twenty pipes of the wine, and let her go. Another was a New England built ship of about 150 tons, bound also home with sugar and molasses, which was good for nothing to us; however, we got near £1,000 on board her in pieces of eight, and taking away her sails as before, brought her to an anchor under the lee of the sloop. At last we met with what we wanted, and this was another ship of about a hundred tons from New England, bound to Barbados. She had on board 150 barrels of flour, about 350 barrels of peas, and ten tons of pork barrelled up and pickled, besides some live hogs and some horses, and six tons of beer.

We were now sufficiently provided for. In all those prizes we got also about fifty-six men, who, by choice and volunteer, agreed to go along with us, including the carpenters and surgeons, who we obliged always to go. So that we were now above 200 men, two ships, and the Bermuda sloop, and giving the other sloop, and the New England homeward-bound ship their sails again, we let them go. And as to the malt, which we took in the Bermuda sloop, we gave it to the last New England master who was going out to Barbados.

We got in all those ships – besides the provisions above-mentioned – about 200 muskets and pistols, good store of cutlasses, about twenty tons of iron shot and musket ball, and thirty-three barrels of good powder, which were all very suitable things to our occasions.

We were fully satisfied, as we said to one another now, and

concluded that we would stand away to the windward as well as we could towards the coast of Africa, that we might come in the wind's way for the coast of Brazil. But our frigate (I mean that we were first shipped in) was yet out upon the cruise and not come in, so we came to an anchor to wait for her, when, behold, the next morning she came in with full sail, and a prize in tow. She had, it seems, been further west than her orders, but had met with a Spanish prize, whither bound or from whence I remember we did not enquire, but we found in her – besides merchandise, which we had no occasion for – 65,000 pieces of eight in silver, some gold, and two boxes of pearl of a good value. Five Dutch, or rather Flemish seamen that were on board her were willing to go with us, and as to the rest of the cargo, we let her go – only finding four of her guns were brass we took them into our ship with seven great jars of powder and some cannon-shot, and let her go, using the Spaniards very civilly.

This was a piece of mere good fortune to us, and was so encouraging as nothing could be more, for it set us up, as we may say; for now we thought we could never fail of good fortune, and we resolved one and all, directly to the South Seas.

It was about the middle of August 1690 that we set forward, and steering E. by S. and E.S.E. for about fifteen days with the winds at N.N.W. variable, we came quickly into the trade winds with a good offing to go clear of all the islands; and so we steered directly for Cape St Augustin in Brazil, which we made the 22nd of September.

We cruised some time upon the coast, about the Bay of All Saints, and put in once or twice for fresh water, especially at the island of St John's, where we got good store of fish, and some hogs, which for fresh provisions was a great relief to us.

But we got no purchase here, for whether it was that their European ships were just come in or just gone out we know not, or whether they suspected what we were, and so kept close within their ports... but in thirteen days that we plied off and on about Pernambuco[7], and about fourteen days more that we spent in coasting along the Brazil shore to the south, we met not one ship, neither saw a sail except of their fishing boats or small coasters, who kept close under shore.

We crossed the line here about the latter end of September and found the air exceeding hot and unwholesome, the sun being in the zenith and the weather very wet and rainy, so we resolved to stand away south without looking for any more purchase on that side.

Accordingly we kept on to the south, having tolerable good weather, and keeping the shore all the way in view till we came the length of St Julien, in the latitude of 48 degrees, twenty-two minutes south. Here we put in again being the beginning of November, and took in fresh water, and spent about ten days refreshing ourselves and fitting our tackle, all which time we lived upon penguins and seals, of which we killed an innumerable number. And when we prepared to go, we salted up as many penguins as we found would serve our whole crew to eat them twice a week as long as they would keep.

Here we consulted together about going through the Straits of Magellan. But I put them quite out of conceit of making that troublesome and fatiguing adventure, the straits being so hazardous and so many winds required to pass them; and having assured them that in our return with Bat Sharp we went away to the latitude of 55 degrees thirty minutes and then steering due east came open with the north seas in five days' run, they all agreed to go that way.

On the 20th November we weighed from Port St Julien, and

having a fair wind at N.E. by E. led it away merrily till we came into the latitude of 54, when the wind veering more northerly and then to the N.W. blowing hard, we were driven into 55 degrees and a half, but lying as near as we could to the wind, we made some westward way withal. The 3rd of December the wind came up south, and S.E. by S. being now just as it were at the beginning of the summer solstice in that country.

With this wind, which blew a fresh gale, we stood away N.N.W. and soon found ourselves in open sea to the west of America, upon which we hauled away N. by E. and N.N.E. and then N.E., when on the 20th of December we made the land – being the coast of Chile – in the latitude of 41 degrees, about the height of Valdivia, and we stood out from hence till we made the isle of St Juan Fernando, where we came to an anchor and went on shore to get fresh water. Also, some of our men went a-hunting for goats, of which we killed enough to feed us all with fresh meat for all the while we stayed here, which was twenty-two days. [Jan. 11.]

During this stay we sent the sloop out to cruise, but she came back without seeing any vessel, after which we ordered her out again more to the north, but she was scarce gone a league when she made a signal that she saw a sail and that we should come out to help them. Accordingly, the frigate put out to sea after them, but making no signal for us to follow we lay still and worked hard at cleaning our ship, shifting some of the rigging and the like.

We heard no more of them in three days, which made us repent sorely that we had not gone all three together. But the third day they came back, though without any prize as we thought, but gave us an account that they had chased a great ship and a bark all night and the next day; that they took the bark the evening before, but found little in her of value; that the great ship ran on shore among some rocks, where they durst not go in after her, but that manning out their boats they got on shore so soon that the men belonging to her durst not land; that then they threatened to burn the ship as she lay, and burn them all in her if they did not come on shore and surrender. They offered to surrender giving them their liberty, which our men would not promise at first. But after some parley and arguing on both sides, our men agreed thus far, that they should remain prisoners for so long as we were in those seas, but that as soon as we came to the height of Panama, or if we resolved to return sooner, then they should be set at liberty. And to these hard conditions they yielded.

Our men found in the ship six brass guns, 200 sacks of meal, some fruit, and the value of 160,000 pieces of eight in gold of Chile, as good as any in the world. It was a glittering sight, and enough to dazzle the eyes of those that looked on it to see such a quantity of gold laid all of a heap together, and we began to embrace one another in congratulation of our good fortune.

We brought the prisoners all to the island Fernando, where we used them very well, built little houses for them, gave them bread and meat and everything they wanted, and gave them powder and ball to kill goats with, which they were fully satisfied with, and killed a great many for us too.

We continued to cruise [Feb. 2] hereabouts, but without finding any other prize for near three weeks more. So we resolved to go up as high as Puno, the place where I had been so lucky before, and we assured our prisoners that in about two months we would return and relieve them. But they chose rather to be on board with us, so we took them all in again and kept on with an easy sail at a proper distance from land, that we might not be known and the alarm given. For as to the ship which we had taken and which was stranded among the rocks – as we had taken all the men out of her, the people on the shore when they should find her could think no other than that she was driven on shore by a storm, and that all the people were drowned, or all escaped and gone. And there was no doubt but that the ship would beat to pieces in a very few days.

We kept, I say, at a distance from the shore, to prevent giving the alarm. But it was a needless caution, for the country was all alarmed on another account, viz. about 130 bold buccaneers had made their way overland, not at the Isthmus of Darien, as usual, but from Granada on the lake of Nicaragua to the north of Panama. By which, though the way was longer and the country not so practicable as at the ordinary passage, yet they were unmolested, for they surprised the country. And whereas the Spaniards looking for them at the old passage had drawn entrenchments, planted guns, and posted men at the passages of the mountains to intercept them and cut them off, here they met with no Spaniards nor any other obstruction in their way, but coming to the South Sea had time, undiscovered, to build themselves canoes and piraguas, and did a great deal of mischief upon the shore, having been followed, among the rest, by eighty men more commanded by one Guilotte, a Frenchman, an old buccaneer: so that they were now 210 men. And they were not long at sea before they took two Spanish barks going from Guatemala to Panama laden with meal, cocoa, and other provisions. So that now they were a fleet of two barks with several canoes and piraguas, but no guns nor any more ammunition than everyone carried at first at their backs.

However, this troop of desperadoes had alarmed all the coast, and expresses both by sea and land were dispatched to warn the towns on the coast to be upon their guard, all the way from Panama to Lima. But as they were represented to be only such freebooters as I have said, ships of strength did not desist their voyages as they found occasion, as we shall observe presently. We were now gotten into the latitude of 10, 11, and 12 degrees and a half, but, in our overmuch caution, had kept out so far to sea that we missed everything which otherwise would have fallen into our hands; but we were better informed quickly, as you shall hear.

Early in the morning one of our men being on the mizen top, cried, '*A sail, a sail!*' It proved to be a small vessel standing just after us, and as we understood afterwards, did so believing that we were some of the King's ships looking after the buccaneers. As we understood she was astern of us, we shortened sail and hung out the Spanish colours, separating ourselves to make him suppose we were cruising for the buccaneers, and did not look for him. However, when we saw him come forward, but stretching in a little towards the shore, we took care to be so much to starboard that he could not escape us that way. And when he was a little nearer, the sloop plainly chased him and in a little time came up with him, and took him. We had little goods in the vessel, their chief loading being meal and corn for Panama, but the master happened to have 6,000 pieces of eight in his cabin, which was good booty.

But that which was better than all this to us was that the master gave us an account of two ships which were behind, and were under sail for Lima or Panama, the one having the revenues of the kingdom of Chile, and the other – having a great quantity of silver – going from Puno to Lima, to be forwarded from thence to Panama, and that they kept together, being ships of force, to protect one another. How they did it we soon saw the effects of.

Upon this intelligence we were very joyful and assured the

master that if we found it so, we would give him his vessel again and all his goods except his money. As for that, we told him such people as we never returned it to anybody. However, the man's intelligence proved good, so the very next day as we were standing south-west, our Spanish colours being out as above, we spied one of the ships and soon after the other. We found they had discovered us also, and that being doubtful what to make of us, they tacked and stood eastward to get nearer the land. We did the like, and as we found there was no letting them go that way but that we should be sure to lose them, we soon let them know that we were resolved to speak with them.

The biggest ship, which was three leagues astern of the other, crowded in for the shore with all the sail she could make, and it was easy for us to see that she would escape us. For as she was a great deal further in with the land than the other when we first gave chase, so in about three hours we saw the land plain ahead of us, and that the great ship would get into port before we could reach her.

Upon this we stretched ahead with all the sail we could make, and the sloop, which crowded also very hard, and outwent us, engaged the small ship at least an hour before we could come up. But she could make little of it, for the Spanish ship having twelve guns and six pedreros[8], would have been too many for the sloop if we had not come up. However, at length, our biggest ship came up also, and, running up under her quarter, gave her our whole broadside, at which she struck immediately, and the Spaniards cried, 'Quarter!' and 'Misericordia!' Upon this, our sloop's men entered her presently and secured her.

In the beginning of this action, it seems, our Redhand captain was so provoked at losing the greater prize, which as

23

◄

he thought had all the money on board, that he swore he would not spare one of the dogs (so he called the Spaniards in the other ship), but he was prevented. And it was very happy for the Spaniards that the first shot the ship made towards us, just as we were running up to pour in our broadside, I say, the first shot took Captain Redhand full on the breast, and shot his head and one shoulder off, so that he never spoke more, nor did I find that any one man in the ship showed the least concern for him. So certain it is, that cruelty never recommends any man among Englishmen, no, though they have no share in the suffering under it. But one said, 'Damn him, let him go, he was a butcherly dog'; another said, 'Damn him, he was a merciless son of a bitch'; another said he was a barbarous dog, and the like.

But to return to the prize, being now as certain of the smaller prize as that we had missed the great one, we began to examine what we had got, and it is not easy to give an exact account of the prodigious variety of things we found. In the first place were 116 chests of pieces of eight in specie, seventy-two bars of silver, fifteen bags of wrought plate (which a friar that was on board would have persuaded us for the sake of the Blessed Virgin to have returned, being, as he said, consecrated plate to the honour of the holy Church, the Virgin Mary, and St Martin – but, as it happened, he could not persuade us to it); also, we found about 6,000 ounces of gold, some in little wedges, some in dust. We found several other things of value, but not to be named with the rest.

Being thus made surprisingly rich, we began to think what course we should steer next. For as the great ship which was escaped would certainly alarm the country, we might be sure we should meet with no more purchase at sea, and we were not very fond of landing to attack any town on shore. In this consultation it is to be observed that I was, by the unanimous consent of all the crew, made captain of the great ship and of the whole crew, the whole voyage hither and every part of it having for some time before been chiefly managed by my direction, or at least by my advice.

The first thing I proposed to them all was, seeing we had met with such good luck, and that we could not expect much more – and if we stayed longer in these seas should find it very hard to revictual our ships, and might have our retreat cut off by Spanish men-of-war (five of which we heard were sent out after the other buccaneers) – we should make the best of our way to the south, and get about into the north seas, where we were out of all danger.

In consequence of this advice, which was generally approved, we stood away directly south, and the wind blowing pretty fair at N.N.E. a merry gale, we stood directly for the isle of Juan Fernando, carrying our rich prize with us.

We arrived here the beginning of June, having been just six months in those seas. We were surprised when coming to the island: we found two ships at an anchor close under the lee of the rocks, and two little piraguas further in near the shore, but being resolved to see what they were, we found to our satisfaction they were the buccaneers of whom I have spoken above. The story is too long to enter upon here, but, in short, without guns, without ship, and only coming overland with their fusils in their hands, they had ranged these seas, had taken several prizes – and some pretty rich – and had got two pretty handsome barks (one carried six guns and the other four). They had shared, as they told us, about 400 pieces of eight a man, besides one thing they had which we were willing to buy of them: they had about a hundred jars of gunpowder, which they took out of a storeship going to Lima.

If we were glad to meet them, you may be sure they were glad to meet with us, and so we began to sort together as one company, only they were loath to give over and return, as we were, and which we had now resolved on.

We were so rich ourselves, and so fully satisfied with what we had taken, that we began to be bountiful to our country-men, and indeed they dealt so generously with us that we could not but be inclined to do them some good, for when we talked of buying their gunpowder they very frankly gave us fifty jars of it gratis.

I took this so kindly that I called a little council among ourselves and proposed to send the poor rogues fifty barrels of our beef, which we could very well spare. And our company agreeing to it, we did so, which made their hearts glad, for it was very good, and they had not tasted good salt beef for a long time – and with it we sent them two hogsheads of rum. This made them so hearty to us that they sent two of their company to compliment us, to offer to enter themselves on board us, and to go with us all the world over.

We did not so readily agree to this at first, because we had no new enterprise in view. But, however, as they sent us word they had chosen me so unanimously for their captain, I proposed to our men to remove ourselves and all our goods into the great ship and the sloop, and so take the honest fellows into the frigate – which now had no less that twenty-two guns, and would hold them all – and then they might sail with us, or go upon any adventures of their own, as we should agree.

Accordingly we did so, and gave them that ship with all her guns and ammunition, but made one of our own men captain, which they consented to, and so we became all one body.

Here also we shared our booty, which was great indeed to a

profusion, and as keeping such a treasure in every man's particular private possession would have occasioned gaming, quarrelling, and perhaps thieving and pilfering, I ordered that so many small chests should be made as there were men in the ship. And every man's treasure was nailed up in these chests, and the chests all stowed in the hold, with every man's name upon his chest, not to be touched but by general order. And to prevent gaming I prevailed with them to make a law or agreement, and everyone to set their hands to it. By which they agreed that, if any man played for any more money than he had in his keeping, the winner should not be paid whatever the loser run in debt, but the chest containing every man's dividend should be all his own to be delivered whole to him. And the offender, whenever he left the ship, if he would pay any gaming debts afterward, that was another case, but such debts should never be paid while he continued in that company.

By this means also we secured the ship's crew keeping together; for if any man left the ship now, he was sure to leave about 6,000 pieces of eight behind him to be shared among the rest of the ship's company, which few of them cared to do.

As we were now all embarked together, the next question was, whither we should go. As for our crew, we were so rich that our men were all for going back again, and so to make off to some of the Leeward Islands, that we might get ashore privately with our booty. But as we had shipped our new comrades on board a good ship, it would be very hard to oblige them to go back without any purchase, for that would be to give them a ship to do them no good but to carry them back to Europe just as they came out from thence, viz. with no money in their pockets.

Upon these considerations we came to this resolution: that

they should go out to sea and cruise the height of Lima and try their fortune, and that we would stay sixty days for them at Juan Fernando.

Upon this agreement they went away very joyful, and we fell to work to new-rig our ship, mending our sails and cleaning our bottom. Here we employed ourselves a month very hard at work; our carpenters also took down some of the ship's upper work, and built it, as we thought, more to the advantage of sailing; so that we had more room within, and yet did not lie so high.

During this time we had a tent set up on shore, and fifty of our men employed themselves wholly in killing goats and fowls for our fresh provisions. And one of our men, under-standing we had some malt left on board the ship which was taken in one of the prizes, set up a great kettle on shore and went to work to brewing and, to our great satisfaction, brewed us some very good beer. But we wanted bottles to keep it in, after it had stood a while in the cask.

However, he brewed us very good small beer, for present use, and instead of hops he found some wild wormwood growing on the island, which gave it no unpleasant taste, and made it very agreeable to us.

Before the time was expired, our frigate sent a sloop to us, which they had taken, to give us notice that they were in a small creek near the mould of the river Guayaquil[9], on the coast of Peru, in the latitude of 22 degrees. They had a great booty in view – there being two ships in the river of Guayaquil, and two more expected to pass by from Lima, in which was a great quantity of plate; that they waited there for them, and begged we would not think the time long, but that if we should go away, they desired that we would fix up a post with a piece of lead on it, signifying where they should come to us, and wherever it was, east or west, north or south, they would follow us with all the sail they could make.

A little while after this, they sent another sloop, which they had taken also, and she brought a vast treasure in silver and very rich goods, which they had got in plundering a town on the continent; and they ordered the sloop to wait for them at the island where we lay, till their return. But they were so eager in the pursuit of their game that they could not think of coming back yet – neither could we blame them, they having such great things in view. So we resolved in pursuit of our former resolution to be gone, and after several consultations among ourselves in what part of the world we should pitch our tent, we broke up at first without any conclusion.

We were all of the opinion that our treasure was so great that, wherever we went, we should be a prey to the government of that place; that it was impossible to go all on shore, and be concealed; and that we should be so jealous of one another that we should certainly betray one another, everyone for fear of his fellow, that is to say, for fear the other should tell first. Some therefore proposed our going about the south point of Cape Horn, and that then going away to the Gulf of Mexico we should go on shore at the Bay of Campeche, and from thence disperse ourselves as well as we could, and everyone go his own way.

I was willing enough to have gone thither because of the treasure I had left there underground. But still I concluded we were (as I have said) too rich to go on shore anywhere to separate, for every man of us had too much wealth to carry about us. And if we separated, the first number of men any of us should meet with that were strong enough to do it would take it from us, and so we should but just expose ourselves to be murdered for that money we had gotten at so much hazard.

Some proposed then our going to the coast of Virginia, and go some on shore in one place, and some in another privately, and so travelling to the seaports where there were most people, we might be concealed, and by degrees reduce ourselves to a private capacity, everyone shifting home as well as they could. This I acknowledged might be done, if we were sure none of us would be false one to another. But while tales might be told, and the teller of the tale was sure to save his own life and treasure and make his peace at the expense of his comrade's, there was no safety. And they might be sure that as the money would render them suspected wherever they came, so they would be examined, and what by faltering in their story and by being cross-examined, kept apart, and the one being made to believe the other had betrayed him and told all, when indeed he might have said nothing to hurt him, the truth of fact would be dragged out by piecemeal, till they would certainly at last come to the gallows.

These objections were equally just to what nation or place soever we could think of going. So that upon the whole, we concluded there was no safety for us but by keeping all together, and going to some part of the world where we might be strong enough to defend ourselves, or be so concealed till we might find out some way of escape that we might not now be so well able to think of.

In the middle of all these consultations – in which I freely own I was at a loss, and could not tell which way to advise – an old sailor stood up and told us, if we would be advised by him, there was a part of the world where he had been, where we might all settle ourselves undisturbed and live very comfortably and plentifully till we could find out some way how to dispose of ourselves better. And that we might easily be strong enough for the inhabitants – who would at first perhaps attack us, but that afterwards they would sort very well with us, and supply us with all sorts of provisions very plentifully. And this was the island of Madagascar. He told us we might live very well there. He gave us a large account of the country, the climate, the people, the plenty of provisions which was to be had there, especially of black cattle, of which he said there was an infinite number and consequently a plenty of milk, of which so many other things were made. In a word, he read us so many lectures upon the goodness of the place and the convenience of living there, that we were one and all eager to go thither, and concluded upon it.

Accordingly, having little left to do (for we had been in a sailing posture some weeks), we left word with the officer who commanded the sloop and with all his men, that they should come after us to Madagascar. And our men were not wanting to let them know all our reasons for going thither, as well as the difficulties we found of going anywhere else, which had so fully possessed them with the hopes of further advantage that they promised for the rest that they would all follow us.

However, as we all calculated the length of the voyage, and that our water and perhaps our provisions might not hold out so far – but especially our water – we agreed that having passed Cape Horn, and got into the north seas, we would steer northward up the east shore of America till we came to St Julien, where we would stay at least fourteen days to take in water, and to store ourselves with seals and penguins, which would greatly eke out our ship's stores. And that then we should cross the great Atlantic Ocean in a milder latitude than if we went directly, and stood immediately over from the passage about the Cape, which must be at least in 55 or 56, and perhaps, as the weather might be, would be in the latitude of 60 or 61.

With this resolution and under these measures, we set sail from the island of St Juan Fernando the 23rd of September (being the same there as our March is here), and keeping the coast of Chile on board, had good weather for about a fortnight, [Octob. 14] till we came into the latitude of 44 degrees south, when finding the wind come equally off the shore from among the mountains, we were obliged to keep further out at sea, where the winds were less uncertain. And some calms we met with, till about the middle of October [16], when the wind springing up at N.N.W. a pretty moderate gale, we jogged S.E. and S.S.E. till we came into the latitude of 55 degrees. And the 16th of November found ourselves in 59 degrees, the weather exceeding cold and severe. But the wind holding fair, we held in with the land, and steering E.S.E. we held that course till we thought ourselves entirely clear of the land, and entered into the north sea, or Atlantic Ocean. And then changing our course we steered N. and N.N.E. but the wind blowing still at N.N.W. a pretty stiff gale, we could make nothing of it till we made the land in the latitude of 52 degrees. And when we came close under shore, we found the winds variable, so we made still N. under the lee of the shore, and made the point of St Julien the 13th of November[10], having been a year and seven days since we parted from thence on our voyage outward-bound.

Here we rested ourselves, took in fresh water and began to kill seals and fowls of several sorts, but especially penguins, which this place is noted for. And here we stayed, in hopes our frigate would arrive, but we heard no news of her; so, at parting, we set up a post, with this inscription, done on a plate of lead, with our names upon the lead, and these words: *Gone to Madagascar, December 10, 1691* (being in that latitude the longest day in the year); – and I doubt not but the post may stand there still.

From hence we launched out into the vast Atlantic Ocean, steering our coast E. by N. and E.N.E. till we had sailed, by our account, about 470 leagues, taking our meridian distance, or departure, from St Julien. And here a strong gale springing up at S.E. by E. and E.S.E. increasing afterwards to a violent storm, we were forced by it to the northward as high as the Tropic, not that it blew a storm all the while, but it blew so steady and so very hard for near twenty days together that we were carried quite out of our intended course. After we had weathered this, we began to recover ourselves again, making still east, and, endeavouring to get to the southward, we had yet another hard gale of wind at S. and S.S.E., so strong that we could make nothing of it at all, whereupon it was resolved, if we could, to make the island of St Helena, which in about three weeks more we very happily came to, on the 17th of January.

It was to our great satisfaction that we found no ships at all here, and we resolved not by any means to let the governor on shore know our ship's name, or any of our officers' names. And I believe our men were very true to one another in that point, but they were not at all shy of letting them know upon what account we were, etc., so that if he could have gotten any of us in his power, as we were afterwards told he endeavoured by two or three ambuscades to do, we should have passed our time but very indifferently. For which, when we went away we let him know we would not have failed to have beaten his little fort about his ears.

We stayed no longer here than just served to refresh ourselves and supply our want of fresh water. The wind presenting fair, Feb. 2 1692, we set sail, and (not to trouble my story with the particulars of the voyage, in which nothing remarkable occurred), we doubled the Cape the 13th of March, and passing on without coming to an anchor or discovering ourselves, we made directly to the island of Madagascar, where we arrived the 7th of April, the sloop – to our particular satisfaction – keeping in company all the way, and bearing the sea as well as our ship upon all occasions.

To this time I had met with nothing but good fortune. Success answered every attempt, and followed every undertaking, and we scarce knew what it was to be disappointed. But we had an interval of our fortune to meet with in this place. We arrived, as above, at the island on the 13th of March[11], but we did not care to make the south part of the island our retreat nor was it a proper place for our business, which was to take possession of a private secure place to make a refuge of. So after staying some time where we put in, which was on the point of land a little to the south of Cape St Augustine[12], and taking in water and provisions there, we stood away to the north, and keeping the island in view, went on till we came to the latitude of 14 degrees. Here we met with a very terrible tornado or hurricane, which, after we had beaten the sea as long as we could, obliged us to run directly for the shore to save our lives as well as we could, in hopes of finding some harbour or bay where we might run in, or at least might go into smooth water till the storm was over.

The sloop was more put to it than we were in the great ship, and being obliged to run afore it a little sooner than we did, she served for a pilot-boat to us which followed. In a word, she ran in under the lee of a great headland, which jetted far out into the sea, and stood very high also, and came to an anchor in three fathoms and a half of water. We followed her but not with the same good luck, though we came to an anchor too, as we thought, safe enough. But the sea going very high, our anchor came home in the night, and we drove on shore in the dark among the rocks in spite of all we were able to do.

Thus we lost the most fortunate ship that ever man sailed with. However, making signals of distress to the sloop, and by the assistance of our own boat we saved our lives, and, the storm abating in the morning, we had time to save many things, particularly our guns, and most of our ammunition. And – which was more than all the rest – we saved our treasure. Though I mention the saving our guns first, yet they were the last things we saved, being obliged to break the upper deck of the ship up for them.

Being thus got on shore, and having built us some huts for our convenience, we had nothing before us but a view of fixing our habitations in the country. For though we had the sloop, we could propose little advantage by her, for as to cruising for booty among the Arabians or Indians, we had neither room for it nor inclination to it, and as for attacking any European ship, the sloop was in no condition to do it, though we had all been on board. For everybody knows that all the ships trading from Europe to the East Indies were ships of force, and too strong for us. So that, in short, we had nothing in view for several months but how to settle ourselves here, and live as comfortably and as well as we could, till something or other might offer for our deliverance.

In this condition we remained on shore above eight months, during which time we built us a little town and fortified it by the direction of one of our gunners, who was a very good engineer, in a very clever and regular manner, placing a very strong double palisado round the foot of our works and a very large ditch without our palisado, and a third palisado beyond the ditch, like a counterscarp or covered way. Besides this, we raised a large battery next to the sea with a line of twenty-one guns placed before it, and thus we thought ourselves in a condition to defend ourselves against any force that could attempt us in that part of the world.

And besides all this, the place on which our habitation was built being an island, there was no coming easily at us by land.

But I was far from being easy in this situation of our affairs. So I made a proposal to our men one day, that though we were well enough in our habitation and wanted for nothing, yet since we had a sloop here – and a boat so good as she was – it was pity she should lie and perish there, but we should send her abroad, and see what might happen; that perhaps it might be our good luck to surprise some ship or other for our turn, and so we might all go to sea again. The proposal was well enough relished at first word, but the great mischief of all was like to be this, that we should go all together by the ears upon the question who should go in her. My secret design was laid that I was resolved to go in her myself, and that she should not go without me. But when it began to be talked of, I discovered the greatest seeming resolution not to stir but to stay with the rest, and take care of the main chance, that was to say, the money.

I found, when they saw that I did not propose to go myself, the men were much the easier. For at first they began to think it was only a project of mine to run away from them, and so indeed it was. However as I did not at first propose to go myself, so when I came to the proposal of who should go, I made a long discourse to them of the obligation they had all to be faithful one to another, and that those who went in the sloop ought to consider themselves and those that were with them to be but one body with those who were left behind; that their whole concern ought to be to get some good ship to fetch them off. At last, I concluded with a proposal that whoever went in the sloop should leave his money behind in the common keeping as it was before, to remain as a pledge for his faithful performing the voyage and coming back again to the company, and should faithfully swear that wherever they went (for as to the voyage, they were at full liberty to go whither they would) they would certainly endeavour to get back to Madagascar; and that if they were cast away, stranded, taken, or whatever befell them, they should never rest till they got to Madagascar, if it was possible.

They all came most readily into this proposal for those who should go into the sloop, but with this alteration in them (which was easy to be seen in their countenances), viz. that from that minute there was no striving who should go, but every man was willing to stay where they were. This was what I wanted, and I let it rest for two or three days, when I took occasion to tell them that, seeing they all were sensible that it was a very good proposal to send the sloop out to sea and see what they could do for us, I thought it was strange they should so generally show themselves backward to the service for fear of parting from their money. I told them that no man need be afraid that the whole body should agree to take his money from him without any pretended offence, much less when he should be abroad for their service. But however, as it was my proposal and I was always willing to hazard myself for the good of them all, so I was ready to go on the conditions I had proposed to them for others, and I was not afraid to flatter myself with serving them so well abroad that they should not grudge to restore me my share of money when I came home, and the like of all those that went with me.

This was so seasonably spoken and humoured so well that it answered my design effectually, and I was voted to go *nemine contradicente*[13]. Then I desired they would draw lots for who and who should go with me, or leave it in my absolute choice to pick and cull my men. They had for some time agreed to the first, and forty blanks were made for those to whose lot it should come to draw a blank to go in the sloop. But then it was said this might neither be a fair nor an effectual choice. For example, if the needful number of officers and of particular occupations should not happen to be lotted out, the sloop might be obliged to go out to sea without a surgeon, or without a carpenter, or without a cook, and the like. So, upon second thoughts, it was left to me to name my men, so I chose me out forty stout fellows, and among them several who were trusty bold men, fit for anything.

Being thus manned, the sloop rigged, and having cleared her bottom and laid in provisions enough for a long voyage, we set sail the 3rd of January 1694[14] for the Cape of Good Hope. We very honestly left our money, as I said, behind us, only that we had about the value of 2,000 pounds in pieces of eight allowed us on board for any exigence that might happen at sea.

We made no stop at the Cape or at St Helena, though we passed in sight of it, but stood over to the Caribbean islands directly, and made the island of Tobago the 18th of February, where we took in fresh water, which we stood in great need of, as you may judge by the length of the voyage. We sought no purchase, for I had fully convinced our men that our business was not to appear as we were used to be upon the cruise, but as traders. And to that end I proposed to go away to the Bay of Campeche and load logwood, under the pretence of selling of which we might go anywhere.

It is true, I had another design here, which was to recover the money which my comrade and I had buried there. And having the man on board with me to whom I had communicated my design, we found an opportunity to come at our money with privacy enough, having so concealed it as that it

38

would have lain there to the general conflagration, if we had not come for it ourselves.

My next resolution was to go for England, only that I had too many men and did not know what to do with them. I told them we could never pretend to go with a sloop laden with logwood to any place with forty men on board, but we should be discovered. But if they would resolve to put fifteen or sixteen men on shore as private seamen, the rest might do well enough, and if they thought it hard to be set on shore, I was content to be one – only that I thought it was very reasonable that whoever went on shore should have some money given them, and that all should agree to rendezvous in England, and so make the best of our way thither, and there perhaps we might get a good ship to go fetch off our comrades and our money. With this resolution, sixteen of our men had 300 pieces of eight a man given them, and they went off thus: the sloop stood away north through the Gulf of Florida, keeping under the shore of Carolina and Virginia; so our men dropped off as if they had deserted the ship; three of the sixteen run away there, five more went off at Virginia, three at New York, three at Rhode Island, and myself and one more at New England; and so the sloop went away for England with the rest. I got all my money on shore with me, and concealed it as well as I could. Some I got bills for, some I bought molasses with, and turned the rest into gold. And dressing myself not as a common sailor but as a master of a ketch which I had lost in the Bay of Campeche, I got passage on board one Captain Guillame, a New England Captain, whose owner was one Mr Johnson, a merchant living at Hackney, near London.

Being at London, it was but a very few months before several of us met again, as I have said we agreed to do. And being true to our first design of going back to our comrades, we had several close conferences about the manner and figure in which we should make the attempt, and we had some very great difficulties appear in our way. First, to have fitted up a small vessel, it would be of no service to us, but be the same thing as the sloop we came in, and if we pretended to a great ship, our money would not hold out. So we were quite at a stand in our councils what to do or what course to take, till at length our money still wasting we grew less able to execute anything we should project.

This made us all desperate. When, as desperate distempers call for desperate cures, I started a proposal which pleased them all – and this was that I would endeavour among my acquaintances and with what money I had left (which was still 1,600 of 1,700 pounds) to get the command of a good ship, bearing a quarter part, or thereabouts, myself. And so having got into the ship and got a freight, the rest of our gang should all enter on board as seamen, and whatever voyage we went, or wheresoever we were bound, we would run away with the ship and all the goods, and so go to our friends as we had promised.

I made several attempts of this kind, and once bought a very good ship called *The Griffin*, off one Snelgrove, a shipwright, and engaged the persons concerned to hold a share in her, and fit her out on a voyage for Leghorn and Venice when it was very probable the cargo – to be shipped on board casually by the merchant – would be very rich. But Providence, and the good fortune of the owner, prevented this bargain, for without any objection against me or discovery of my design in the least, he told me afterwards his wife had an ugly dream or two about the ship – once, that it was set on fire by lightning and he had lost all he had in it; another time, that the men had mutinied and conspired to kill him – and that his wife was so averse to his being concerned in it that it had always been an unlucky ship, and that therefore his mind was changed; that he would sell the whole ship, if I would, but he would not hold any part of it himself.

Though I was very much disappointed at this, yet I put a very good face upon it and told him I was very glad to hear him tell me particulars of his dissatisfaction. For if there was anything in dreams and his wife's dream had any signification at all, it seemed to concern me (more than him) who was to go the voyage and command the ship. And whether the ship was to be burnt or the men to mutiny, though part of the loss might be his, who was to stay on shore, all the danger was to be mine, who was to be at sea in her. And then if, as he had said, she had been an unlucky ship to him, it was very likely she would be so to me; and therefore I thanked him for the discovery, and told him I would not meddle with her.

The man was uneasy and began to waver in his resolution and had it not been for the continued importunities of his wife, I believe, would have come on again – for people generally incline to a thing that is rejected when they would reject the same thing when proffered. But I knew it was not my business to let myself be blowed upon, so I kept to my resolution and wholly declined that affair, on pretence of its having got an ill name for an unlucky ship. And that name stuck so to her that the owners could never sell her, and as I have been informed since, were obliged to break her up at last.

It was a great while I spent with hunting after a ship but was every way disappointed, till money grew short and the number of my men lessened apace, and at last we were reduced to seven, when an opportunity happened in my way to go chief mate on board a stout ship bound from London to —

[NB In things so modern, it is no way convenient to write to

41

you particular circumstances and names of persons, ships, or places because those things being in themselves criminal, may be called up in question in a judicial way. And therefore I warn the reader to observe that not only all the names are omitted but even the scene of action in this criminal part is not laid exactly as things were acted, lest I should give justice a clue to unravel my story by, which nobody will blame me for avoiding.]

It is enough to tell the reader that being put out to sea, and being for convenience of wind and weather come to an anchor on the coast of Spain, my seven companions having resolved upon our measures and having brought three more of the men to confederate with us, we took up arms in the middle of the night, secured the captain, the gunner, and the carpenter, and after that all the rest of the men, and declared our intention. The captain and nine men refused to come into our projected roguery (for we gave them their choice to go with us, or go on shore), so we put them on shore very civilly, gave the master his books, and everything he could carry with him, and all the rest of the men agreed to go along with us.

As I had resolved before I went on board upon what I purposed to do, so I had laid out all the money I had left in such things as I knew I should want, and had caused one of my men to pretend he was going to — to build or buy a ship there, and that he wanted freight for a great deal of cordage, anchors, eight guns, powder and ball, with about twenty tons of lead and other bulky goods, which were all put on board as merchandise.

We had not abundance of bale goods on board, which I was glad of; not that I made any conscience or scruple of carrying them away, if the ship had been full of them, but we had no market for them. Our first business was to get a larger store of provisions on board than we had, our voyage being long, and having acquainted the men with our design, and promised the new men a share of the wealth we had there, which made them very hearty to us, we set sail. We took in some beef and fish at — where we lay fifteen days, but out of all reach of the castle or fort, and having done our business sailed away for the Canaries, where we took in some butts of wine, and some fresh water. With the guns the ship had and those eight I had put on board as merchandise, we had then two and thirty guns mounted but were but slenderly manned, though we got four English seamen at the Canaries. But we made up the loss at Faial (island), where we made bold with three English ships we found, and partly by fair means and partly by force, shipped twelve men there, after which, without any further stop for men or stores, we kept the coast of Africa on board till we passed the line and then stood off to St Helena.

Here we took in fresh water and some fresh provisions, and went directly for the Cape of Good Hope, which we passed, stopping only to fill about twenty-two butts of water, and with a fair gale entered the sea of Madagascar. And sailing up the west shore between the island and the coast of Africa, came to an anchor over against our settlement, about two leagues' distance, and made the signal of our arrival with firing twice seven guns at the distance of a two-minute glass between the seven; when, to our infinite joy, the fort answered us and the longboat, the same that belonged to our former ship, came off to us.

We embraced one another with inexpressible joy, and the next morning I went on shore. And our men brought our ship safe into harbour – laying within the defence of our platform, and within two cables' length of the shore, good soft ground, and in eleven fathom water – having been three months and eighteen days on the voyage, and almost three years absent from the place.

When I came to look about me here, I found our men had increased their number, and that a vessel which had been cruising, that is to say pirating on the coast of Arabia, having seven Dutchmen, three Portuguese and five Englishmen on board, had been cast away upon the northern shore of that island, and had been taken up and relieved by our men, and lived among them. They told us also of another crew of European sailors, which lay as we did on the main of the island, and had lost their ship, and were, as the islanders told them, above a hundred men, but we heard nothing who they were.

Some of our men were dead in the meantime, I think about three; and the first thing I did was to call a muster, and see how things stood as to money. I found the men had been very true to one another; there lay all the money in chests piled up as I left it, and every man's money having his name upon it. Then acquainting the rest with the promise I had made the men that came with me, they all agreed to it: so the money belonging to the dead men and to the rest of the forty men who belonged to the sloop was divided among the men I brought with me, as well those who joined at first as those we took in at the Cape de Verde, and the Canaries. And the bales of goods which we found in the ship – many of which were valuable for our own use – we agreed to give them all to the fifteen men mentioned above who had been saved by our men, and so to buy what we wanted of those goods off them, which made their hearts glad also.

And now we began to consult what course to take in the world. As for going to England, though our men had a great mind to be there, yet none of them knew how to get thither, notwithstanding I had brought them a ship; but I, who had now made myself too public to think any more of England, had given over all views that way, and began to cast about for further adventures. For though, as I said, we were immensely rich before, yet I abhorred lying still and burying myself alive, as I called it, among savages and barbarians. Besides, some of our men were young in the trade and had seen nothing; and they lay at me every day not to lie still in a part of the world where, as they said, such vast riches might be gained. And that the Dutchmen and Englishmen who were cast away, as above, and who our men called the *comelings*, were continually buzzing in my ears what infinite wealth was to be got if I would but make one voyage to the coast of Madagascar, Coromandel[15], and the Bay of Bengal. Nay, the three Portuguese seamen offered themselves to attack and bring off one of their biggest galleons, even out of the road of Goa on the Malabar coast, the capital of the Portuguese factories in the Indies.

In a word, I was overcome with these new proposals, and told the rest of my people I was resolved to go to sea again and try my good fortune; I was sorry I had not another ship or two, but if ever it lay in my power to master a good ship I would not fail to bring her to them.

While I was thus fitting out upon this new undertaking, and the ship lay ready to sail – and all the men who were designed for the voyage were on board, being eighty-five in number, among which were all the men I brought with me, the fifteen comelings, and the rest made up out of our old number – I say, when I was just upon the point of setting sail, we were all surprised just in the grey of the morning to spy a sail at sea. We knew not what to make of her, but found she was a European ship, that she was not a very large vessel, yet that she was a ship of force too. She seemed to shorten sail, as if she looked out for some harbour. At first sight I thought she was English:

immediately I resolved to slip anchor and cable and go out to sea and speak with her, if I could, let her be what she would. As soon as I was got a little clear of the land, I fired a gun and spread English colours. She immediately brought to, fired three guns, and manned out her boat with a flag of truce. I did the like, and the two boats spoke to one another in about two hours, when, to our infinite joy, we found they were our comrades who we left in the South Seas, and to whom we gave the frigate at the isle of Juan Fernando.

Nothing of this kind could have happened more to our mutual satisfaction, for though we had long ago given them over either for lost, or lost to us, and we had no great need of company, yet we were overjoyed at meeting and so were they too.

They were in some distress for provisions and we had plenty. So we brought their ship in for them, gave them a present supply, and when we had helped them to moor and secure the ship in the harbour, we made them lock all their hatches and cabins up and come on shore; and there we feasted them five or six days, for we had a plenty of all sorts of provisions, not to be exhausted – and if we had wanted a hundred heads of fat bullocks, we could have had them for asking for of the natives, who treated us all along with all possible courtesy and freedom in their way.

The history of the adventures and successes of these men, from the time we left them to the time of their arrival at our new plantation, was our whole entertainment for some days. I cannot pretend to give the particulars by my memory; but as they came to us thieves, they improved in their calling to a great degree, and, next to ourselves, had the greatest success of any of the buccaneers whose story has ever been made public.

I shall not take upon me to vouch the whole account of their actions, neither will this letter contain a full history of their adventures, but if the account which they gave us was true, you may take it thus.

First, that having met with good success after they left us, and having taken some extraordinary purchase – as well in some vessels they took at sea, as in the plunder of some towns on the shore near Guayaquil, as I have already told you – they got information of a large ship which was loading the King's money at Puno and had orders to sail with it to Lima, in order to its being carried from thence to Panama by the fleet under the convoy of the flotilla, or squadron of men-of-war, which the King's Governor at Panama had sent to prevent their being insulted by pirates (which they had intelligence were on the coast; by which, we suppose, they meant us who were gone, for they could have no notion of these men then).

Upon this intelligence they cruised off and on upon the coast for near a month, keeping always to the southward of Lima, because they would not fall in the way of the said flotilla, and so be overpowered and miss of their prize. At last they met with what they looked for, that is to say, they met with the great ship above-named. But to their great misfortune and disappointment (as they first thought it to be), she had with her a man-of-war for her convoy and two other merchant ships in her company.

The buccaneers had with them the sloop which they first sent to us for our intelligence, and which they made a little frigate of, carrying eight guns, and some pedreros. They had not long time to consult, but in short they resolved to double-man the sloop and let her attack the great merchant ship, while the frigate – which was the whole of their fleet – held the man-of-war in play, or at least kept him from assisting her.

According to this resolution they put fifty men on board the sloop, which was, in short, almost as many as would stand upon her deck one by another; and with this force they attacked the great merchant ship, which, besides its being well-manned, had sixteen good guns, and about thirty men on board. While the sloop thus began the unequal fight, the man-of-war bore down upon her to succour the ship under her convoy, but the frigate thrusting in between engaged the man-of-war and began a very warm fight with her, for the man-of-war had both more guns and more men than the frigate after she had parted with fifty men on board the sloop. While the two men-of-war, as we may now call them, were thus engaged, the sloop was in great danger of being worsted by the merchant ship, for the force was too much for her, the ship was great and her men fought a desperate and close fight. Twice the sloop men entered her and were beaten off and about nine of their men killed, several others wounded, and, an unlucky shot taking the sloop between wind and water, she was obliged to fall astern, and heel her over to stop the leak – during which the Spaniards steered away to assist the man-of-war, and poured her broadside in upon the frigate, which though but small, yet at a time when she lay yardarm and yardarm close by the side of the Spanish man-of-war, was a great extremity. However, the frigate returned her broadside and therewith made her sheer off, and, which was worse, shot her mainmast through, though it did not come presently by the board.

During this time, the sloop, having many hands, had stopped the leak, was brought to rights again, and came up again to the engagement, and at the first broadside had the good luck to bring the ship's foremast by the board and thereby disabled her, but could not, for all that, lay her athwart or carry her by boarding, so that the case began to be very doubtful. At which, the captain of the sloop, finding the merchant ship was disabled and could not get away from them, resolved to leave her a while and assist the frigate – which he did. And running alongside our frigate, he fairly laid the man-of-war on board just athwart his hawser[16], and besides firing into her with his great shot, he very fairly set her on fire; and it was a great chance but that they had been all three burnt together, but our men helped the Spaniards themselves to put out the fire and after some time mastered it. But the Spaniards were in such a terrible fright at the apprehension of the fire that they made little resistance afterwards, and in short, in about an hour's fight more, the Spanish man-of-war struck and was taken. And after that the merchant ship also, with all the wealth that was in her. And thus their victory was as complete as it was unexpected.

The captain of the Spanish man-of-war was killed in the fight and about thirty-six of his men, and most of the rest wounded, which it seems happened upon the sloop's lying athwart her. This man-of-war was a new ship, and with some alteration in her upper work made a very good frigate for them, and they afterwards quitted their own ship and went all on board the Spanish ship, taking out the mainmast of their own ship and making a new foremast for the Spanish ship, because her foremast was also weakened with some shot in her. This, however, cost them a great deal of labour and difficulty and also some time, when they came to a certain creek where they all went on shore and refreshed themselves a while.

But if the taking of the man-of-war was an unexpected victory to them, the wealth of the prize was much more so, for they found an amazing treasure on board her both in silver and gold – and the account they gave me was but imperfect – but I think they calculated the pieces of eight to be about thirteen tons in weight; besides that they had five small chests of gold, some emeralds and, in a word, a prodigious booty.

They were not, however, so modest in their prosperity as we were. For they never knew when to have done but they must cruise again to the northward for more booty, when to their great surprise they fell in with the flotilla or squadron of men-of-war which they had so studiously avoided before, and were so surrounded by them that there was no remedy but they must fight – and that in a kind of desperation, having no prospect now but to sell their lives as dear as they could.

This unlucky accident befell them before they had changed their ship, so that they had now the sloop and both the men-of-war in company, but they were but thinly manned; as for the booty, the greater part of it was on board the sloop, that is to say, all the gold and emeralds, and near half the silver.

When they saw the necessity of fighting, they ordered the sloop, if possible, to keep to windward so that she might, as night came on, make the best of her way and escape. But a Spanish frigate of eighteen guns tended her so close and sailed so well that the sloop could by no means get away from the rest, so she made up close to the buccaneers' frigate and maintained a fight as well as she could, till in the dusk of the evening the Spaniards boarded and took her, but most of her men got away in her boat, and some by swimming on board the other ship. They only left in her five wounded Englishmen and six Spanish Negroes. The five English the barbarous Spaniards hanged up immediately, wounded as they were.

This was good notice to the other men to tell them what they were to expect, and made them fight like desperate men till night, and killed the Spaniards a great many men. It proved a very dark rainy night, so that the Spaniards were obliged by necessity to give over the fight till the next day, endeavouring, in the meantime, to keep as near them as they could. But the buccaneers, concerting their measures where they should meet, resolved to make use of the darkness of the night to get off if they could, and the wind springing up a fresh gale at S.S.W. they changed their course, and, with all the sail they could make, stood away to the N.N.W. slanting it to seawards as nigh the wind as they could. And getting clear away from the Spaniards – who they never saw more – they made no stay till they passed the line and arrived in about twenty-two days' sail on the coast of California, where they were quite out of the way of all enquiry and search of the Spaniards.

Here it was they changed their ship as I said, and, quitting their own vessel, they went all on board the Spanish man-of-war, fitting up her masts and rigging, as I have said, and taking out all the guns, stores, etc. of their own ship, so that they had now a stout ship under them, carrying forty guns (for so many they made her carry), and well furnished with all things. And though they had lost so great a part of their booty, yet they had still left a vast wealth, being six or seven tons of silver, besides what they had gotten before.

With this booty (and regretting heartily they had not prac-tised the same moderation before), they resolved now to be satisfied and make the best of their way to the island of Juan Fernando, where keeping at a great distance from the shore, they safely arrived in about two months' voyage, having met with some contrary winds by the way.

However, here they found the other sloop which they had sent in with their first booty, to wait for them. And here, understanding that we were gone for St Julien, they resolved (since the time was so long gone that they could not expect to find us again) that they would have the other touch with the Spaniards, cost what it would. And accordingly, having first buried the most part of their money in the ground on shore in the island, and having revictualled their ship in the best manner they could in that barren island, away they went to sea.

They beat about on the south of the line all up the coast of Chile and part of Peru, till they came to the height of Lima itself.

They met with several ships and took several, but they were laden chiefly with lumber or provisions – except that in one vessel they took between 40 and 50,000 pieces of eight, and in another 75,000. They soon informed themselves that the Spanish men-of-war were gone out of those seas up to Panama to boast of their good fortune, and carry home their prize – and this made them the bolder. But though they spent near five months in this second cruise, they met with nothing considerable, the Spaniards being everywhere alarmed, and having notice of them so that nothing stirred abroad.

Tired then with their long cruise and out of hope of more booty, they began to look homeward and to say to one another that they had enough. So, in a word, they came back to Juan Fernando, and there furnishing themselves as well as they could with provisions and not forgetting to take their treasure on board with them, they set forward again to the south. And, after a very bad voyage in rounding the Terra del Fuego – being driven to the latitude of 65 degrees, where they felt extremity of cold – they at length obtained a more favourable wind, viz. at S. and S.S.E. with which, steering to the north, they came into a milder sea and a milder coast, and at length arrived at Port St Julien, where to their great joy they found the post or cross erected by us. And understanding that we were gone to Madagascar and that we would be sure to remain there to hear from them, and withal that we had been gone there near two years, they resolved to follow us.

Here they stayed, it seems, almost half a year, partly fitting and altering their ship, partly wearing out the winter season and waiting for milder weather. And having victualled their ship in but a very ordinary manner for so long a run, viz. only with seals' flesh and penguins and some deer they killed in the country, they at last launched out, and crossing the great Atlantic Ocean, they made the Cape of Good Hope in about seventy-six days, having been put to very great distresses in that time for want of food (all their seals' flesh and penguins growing nauseous and stinking in little less than half the time of their voyage; so that they had nothing to subsist on for seven and twenty days but a little quantity of dried venison which they killed on shore, about the quantity of three barrels of English beef, and some bread). And when they came to the Cape of Good Hope, they got some small supply, but it being soon perceived on shore what they were, they were glad to be gone as soon as they had filled their casks with water, and got but a very little provisions. So they made to the coast of Natal on the south-east point of Africa, and there they got more fresh provisions, such as veal, milk, goats' flesh, some tolerable butter and very good beef. And this held them out till they found us in the north part of Madagascar, as above.

We stayed about a fortnight in our port and in a sailing posture, just as if we had been wind-bound, merely to con-gratulate and make merry with our new-come friends, when I resolved to leave them there and set sail – which I did with a westerly wind, keeping away north till I came into the latitude of seven degrees north. So coasting along the Arabian coast E.N.E. towards the Gulf of Persia, in the cruise I met with two Persian barks laden with rice, one of which I manned and sent away to Madagascar, and the other I took for our own ship's use. This bark came safe to my new colony, and was a very agreeable prize to them; I think verily almost as agreeable as if it had been loaded with pieces of eight, for they had been without bread a great while. And this was a double benefit to them, for they fitted up this bark, which carried about fifty-five tons, and went away to the Gulf of Persia in her to buy rice, and brought two or three freights of that, which was very good.

In this time I pursued my voyage, coasted the whole Malabar shore and met with no purchase but a great Portugal East India ship, which I chased to Goa, where she got out of my reach. I took several small vessels and barks, but little of value in them, till I entered the great Bay of Bengal, when I began to look about me with more expectation of success, though without prospect of what happened.

I cruised here about two months, finding nothing worthwhile. So I stood away to a port on the north point of the isle of Sumatra, where I made no stay. For here I got news that two large ships belonging to the Great Mogul were expected to cross the bay from Hooghly in the Ganges to the country of the King of Pegu[17], being to carry the granddaughter of the Great Mogul to Pegu – who was to be married to the King of that country – with all her retinue, jewels, and wealth.

This was a booty worth watching for, though it had been some months longer. So I resolved that we would go and cruise off of Point Negaris, on the east side of the bay, near Diamond Isle. And here we plied off and on for three weeks and began to despair of success. But the knowledge of the booty we expected spurred us on, and we waited with great patience for we knew the prize would be immensely rich.

At length we spied three ships coming right up to us with the wind. We could easily see they were not Europeans by their sails, and began to prepare ourselves for a prize, not for a fight, but were a little disappointed when we found the first ship full of guns and full of soldiers, and in condition – had she been managed by English sailors – to have fought two such ships as ours were. However, we resolved to attack her if she had been full of devils as she was full of men.

Accordingly, when we came near them we fired a gun with shot as a challenge. They fired again immediately three or four guns, but fired them so confusedly that we could easily see they did not understand their business; when we considered how to lay them on board and so to come athwart them, if we could, but falling, for want of wind, open to them we gave them a fair broadside. We could easily see by the confusion that was on board that they were frighted out of their wits: they fired here a gun and there a gun, and some on that side that was from us, as well as those that were next to us. The next thing we did was to lay them on board, which we did presently, and then gave them a volley of our small shot, which, as they stood so thick, killed a great many of them, and made all the rest run down under their hatches crying out like creatures bewitched. In a word, we presently took the ship, and having secured her men, we chased the other two. One was chiefly filled with women, and the other with lumber. Upon the whole, as the granddaughter of the Great Mogul was our prize in the first ship, so in the second was her women, or, in a word, her household, her eunuchs, all the necessaries of her wardrobe, of her stables, and of her kitchen; and in the last, great quantities of household stuff and things less costly, though not less useful.

But the first was the main prize. When my men had entered and mastered the ship, one of our lieutenants called for me and accordingly I jumped on board. He told me he thought nobody but I ought to go into the great cabin, or, at least, nobody should go there before me, for the lady herself and all her attendance was there, and he feared the men were so heated they would murder them all, or do worse.

I immediately went to the great cabin door, taking the lieutenant that called me along with me, and caused the cabin door to be opened. But such a sight of glory and misery was never seen by buccaneer before. The Queen (for such she was to have been) was all in gold and silver, but frighted and crying, and at the sight of me she appeared trembling and just as if she was going to die. She sat on the side of a kind of a bed, like a couch with no canopy over it, or any covering, only made to lie down upon. She was, in a manner, covered with diamonds, and I, like a true pirate, soon let her see that I had more mind to the jewels than to the lady.

However, before I touched her, I ordered the lieutenant to place a guard at the cabin door and, fastening the door, shut us both in, which he did. The lady was young, and, I suppose, in their country esteem very handsome, but she was not very much so in my thoughts. At first, her fright and the danger she thought she was in of being killed taught her to do everything that she thought might interpose between her and danger, and that was to take off her jewels as fast as she could, and give them to me. And I, without any great compliment, took them as fast as she gave them to me and put them into my pocket, taking no great notice of them or of her, which frighted her worse than all the rest, and she said something which I could not understand. However, two of the other ladies came, all crying, and kneeled down to me with their hands lifted up. What they meant I knew not at first, but by their gestures and pointings I found at last it was to beg the young Queen's life, and that I would not kill her.

I have heard that it has been reported in England that I

ravished this lady and then used her most barbarously, but they wrong me, for I never offered anything of that kind to her, I assure you. Nay, I was so far from being inclined to it that I did not like her, and there was one of her ladies who I found much more agreeable to me and who I was afterwards something free with, but not even with her either by force, or by way of ravishing.

We did, indeed, ravish them of all their wealth, for that was what we wanted, not the women. Nor was there any other ravishing among those in the great cabin, that I can assure you. As for the ship where the women of inferior rank were, and who were in number almost two hundred, I cannot answer for what might happen in the first heat. But even there, after the first heat of our men was over, what was done was done quietly, for I have heard some of the men say that there was not a woman among them but that was lain with four or five times over, that is to say, by so many several men. For as the women made no opposition, so the men even took those that were next them, without ceremony, when and where opportunity offered.

When the three ladies kneeled down to me, and as soon as I understood what it was for, I let them know I would not hurt the Queen nor let anyone else hurt her, but that she must give me all her jewels and money. Upon this they acquainted her that I would save her life, and no sooner had they assured her of that but she got up, smiling, and went to a fine Indian cabinet and opened a private drawer, from whence she took another little thing full of little square drawers and holes: this she brings to me in her hand, and offered to kneel down to give it me. This innocent usage began to rouse some good nature in me (though I never had much), and I would not let her kneel but, sitting down myself on the side of her couch or bed, made a motion to her to sit down too. But here she was frighted again, it seems, at what I had no thought of, for sitting on her bed, she thought I would pull her down to lie with her and so did all her women too, for they began to hold their hands before their faces which, as I understood afterwards, was that they might not see me turn up their Queen. But as I did not offer anything of that kind, only made her sit down by me, they began all to be easier after some time and she gave me the little box or casket (I know not what to call it), but it was full of invaluable jewels. I have them still in my keeping, and wish they were safe in England, for I doubt not but some of them are fit to be placed on the King's crown.

Being master of this treasure, I was very willing to be good-humoured to the persons, so I went out of the cabin and caused the women to be left alone, causing the guard to be kept still – that they might receive no more injury than I would do them myself.

After I had been out of the cabin some time, a slave of the women's came to me and made sign to me that the Queen would speak with me again. I made signs back that I would come and dine with her majesty. And accordingly I ordered that her servants should prepare her dinner and carry it in, and then call me. They provided her repast after the usual manner, and, when she saw it brought in, she appeared pleased, and more when she saw me come in after it, for she was exceedingly pleased that I had caused a guard to keep the rest of my men from her, and she had, it seems, been told how rude they had been to some of the women that belonged to her.

When I came in, she rose up and paid me such respect as I did not well know how to receive, and not in the least how to return. If she had understood English, I could have said plainly, and in good rough words, 'Madam, be easy, we are rude rough-hewn fellows, but none of our men should hurt you, or touch you; I will be your guard and protection; we are for money, indeed, and we shall take what you have, but we will do you no other harm.' But as I could not talk thus to her, I scarce knew what to say, but I sat down, and made signs to have her sit down and eat, which she did, but with so much ceremony that I did not know well what to do with it.

After we had eaten, she rose up again and, drinking some water out of a china cup, sat down on the side of the couch as before. When she saw I had done eating, she went then to another cabinet, and pulling out a drawer she brought it to me. It was full of small pieces of gold coin of Pegu, about as big as an English half-guinea, and I think there were 3,000 of them. She opened several other drawers and showed me the wealth that was in them, and then gave me the key of the whole.

We had revelled thus all day and part of the next day in a bottomless sea of riches, when my lieutenant began to tell me we must consider what to do with our prisoners and the ships, for that there was no subsisting in that manner. Besides, he hinted privately that the men would be ruined by lying with the women in the other ship, where all sorts of liberty was both given and taken. Upon this we called a short council and concluded to carry the great ship away with us, but to put all the prisoners, Queen, ladies, and all the rest into the lesser vessels, and let them go. And so far was I from ravishing this lady – as I hear is reported of me – that though I might rifle her of everything else, yet I assure you I let her go untouched for me, or, as I am satisfied, for anyone of my men. Nay, when we dismissed them, we gave her leave to take a great many things of value with her, which she would have been plundered of, if I had not been so careful of her.

We had now wealth enough not only to make us rich but almost to have made a nation rich, and to tell you the truth – considering the costly things we took here, which we did not know the value of, and besides gold, and silver, and jewels – I say, we never knew how rich we were. Besides which, we had a great quantity of bales of goods, as well calicoes as wrought silks which, being for sale, were perhaps as a cargo of goods to answer the bills which might be drawn upon them for the account of the bride's portion – all which fell into our hands, with a great sum in silver coin, too big to talk of among Englishmen, especially while I am living, for reasons which I may give you hereafter.

I had nothing to do now but to think of coming back to Madagascar, so we made the best of our way, only that, to make us quite distracted without other joy, we took in our way a small bark laden with arrack and rice, which was good sauce to our other purchase. For if the women made our men drunk before, this arrack made them quite mad. And they had so little government of themselves with it that I think it might be said the whole ship's crew was drunk for above a fortnight together, till six or seven of them killed themselves, two fell overboard and were drowned, and several more fell into raging fevers – and it was a wonder, in the whole, they were not all killed with it.

But to make short of the story as we did of the voyage, we had a very pleasant voyage, except those disasters, and we came safe back to our comrades at Madagascar, having been absent in all about seven months.

We found them in very good health, and longing to hear from us. And we were, you may be assured, welcome to them, for now we had amassed such a treasure as no society of man ever possessed in this world before us, neither could we ever bring it to an estimation, for we could not bring particular things to a just valuation.

We lived now and enjoyed ourselves in full security, for though some of the European nations, and perhaps all of them had heard of us, yet they heard such formidable things of us, such terrible stories of our great strength as well as of our great wealth, that they had no thought of undertaking anything against us. For, as I have understood, they were told at London that we were no less than 5,000 men; that we had built a regular fortress for our defence by land, and that we had twenty sail of ships. And I have been told that in France they have heard the same thing. But nothing of all this was ever true, any more than it was true that we offered ten million to the government of England for our pardon.

It is true that, had the Queen sent any intimation to us of a pardon and that we should have been received to grace at home, we should all have very willingly embraced it. For we had money enough to have encouraged us all to live honest and, if we had been asked for a million pieces of eight, or a million of pounds sterling, to have purchased our pardon, we should have been very ready to have complied with it, for we really knew not what to do with ourselves or with our wealth. And the only thing we had now before us was to consider what method to take for getting home, if possible, to our own country with our wealth, or at least with such part of it as would secure us easy and comfortable lives. And for my own part I resolved, if I could, to make full satisfaction to all the persons who I had wronged in England, I mean by that, such people as I had injured by running away with the ship, as well the owners, and the master or captain who I set ashore in Spain, as the merchant whose goods I had taken with the ship. And I was daily forming schemes in my thoughts how to bring this to pass. But we all concluded that it was impossible for us to accomplish our desires as to that part, seeing the fact of our piracy was now so public all over the world that there was not any nation in the world that would receive us, or any of us, but would immediately seize on our wealth and execute us for pirates and robbers of all nations.

This was confirmed to us after some time, with all the particulars, as it is now understood in Europe. For as the fame of our wealth and power was such that it made all the world afraid of us, so it brought some of the like sort with ourselves to join with us from all parts of the world. And particularly, we had a bark and sixty men of all nations from Martinique, who had been cruising in the Gulf of Florida, come over to us to try if they could mend their fortunes – and these went afterwards to the Gulf of Persia, where they took some prizes, and returned to us again. We had after this three pirate ships come to us, most English, who had done some exploits on the coast of Guinea, had made several good prizes and were all tolerably rich.

As these people came and sheltered with us, so they came and went as they would – and sometimes some of our men went with them, sometimes theirs stayed with us. But by that coming and going our men found ways and means to convey themselves away, some one way, some another. For I should have told you, at first, that after we had such intelligence from England, viz. that they knew of all our successful enterprises, and that there was no hopes of our returning – especially of mine and some other men who were known – I say, after this we called a general council to consider what to do. And there, one and all, we concluded that we lived very happy where we were, that if any of us had a mind to venture to get away to any part of the world none should hinder them, but that else we would continue where we were. And that the first opportunity we had we would cruise upon the English East India ships and do them what spoil we could, fancying that some time or other they would proclaim a pardon to us if we would come in and, if they did, then we would accept of it.

Under these circumstances we remained here, off and on, first and last, above three years more; during which time our number increased so, especially at first, that we were once 800 men, stout brave fellows and as good sailors as any in the world. Our number decreased afterwards upon several occasions, such as the going abroad to cruise, wandering to the south part of the island, (as above) getting on board European ships, and the like.

After I perceived that a great many of our men were gone off and had carried their wealth with them, I began to cast about in my own thoughts how I should make my way home also. Innumerable difficulties presented to my view, when at last an account of some of our men's escape into Persia encouraged me. The story was this. One of the small barks we had taken went to Gujarat to get rice, and having secured a cargo but not loaded it, ten of our men resolved to attempt their escape. And accordingly they dressed themselves like merchant strangers and bought several sorts of goods there, such as an Englishman, who they found there, assisted them to buy. And with their bales (but in them packed up all the rest of their money) they went up to Bassora[18] in the Gulf of Persia, and so travelled as merchants with the caravan to Aleppo, and we never heard any more of them, but that they went clean off with all their cargo.

This filled my head with schemes for my own deliverance but, however, it was a year more before I attempted anything, and not till I found that many of our men shifted off, some and some, nor did any of them miscarry – some went one way, some another; some lost their money, and some saved it; nay, some carried it away with them, and some left it behind them. As for me, I discovered my intentions to nobody, but made them all believe I would stay here till some of them should come and fetch me off, and pretended to make every man that went off promise to come for me if it was ever in his power, and gave every one of them signals to make for me when they came back, upon which I would certainly come off to them. At the same time nothing was more certain than that I intended from the beginning to get away from the island, as soon as I could any way make my way with safety to any part of the world.

It was still above two years after this that I remained in the island, nor could I, in all that time, find any probable means for removing myself with safety.

One of the ways I thought to have made my escape was this. I went to sea in a longboat a-fishing (as we often did) and having a sail to the boat, we were out two or three days together. At length it came into my thoughts that we might cruise about the island in this longboat a great way, and perhaps some adventure might happen to us which we might make something of. So I told them I had a mind to make a voyage with the longboat to see what would happen.

To this purpose we built upon her, made a stateroom in the middle and clapped four pedreros upon her gunnel, and away we went, being sixteen stout fellows in the boat, not reckoning myself. Thus we ran away, as it were, from the rest of our crew, though not a man of us knew our own minds as to whither we were going or upon what design. In this frolic we ran south quite away to the Bay of St Augustine's, in the latitude of 24 degrees, where the ships from Europe often put in for water and provisions.

Here we put in, not knowing well what to do next. I thought myself disappointed very much that we saw no European ship here, though afterwards I saw my mistake and found that it was better for us that we were in that port first. We went boldly on shore – for as to the natives, we understood how to manage them well enough, knew all their customs and the manner of their treating with strangers as to peace or war, their temper and how to oblige them, or behave if they were disobliged. So we went, I say, boldly on shore, and there we began to chaffer with them for some provisions, such as we wanted.

We had not been here above two or three days but that, early in the morning, the weather thick and hazy, we heard several guns fire at sea. We were not at a loss to know what they meant, and that it was certainly some European ships coming in, and who gave the signal to one another that they had made the land (which they could easily see from the sea, though we, who were also within the bay, could not see them from the shore). However, in a few hours, the weather clearing up, we saw plainly five large ships, three with English colours and two with Dutch, standing into the bay, and in about four of five hours more they came to an anchor.

A little while after they were come to an anchor, their boats began to come on shore to the usual watering place to fill their casks, and while they were doing that, the rest of the men looked about them a little as usual, though at first they did not stir very far from their boats.

I had now as nice a game to play as any man in the world ever had. It was absolutely necessary for us to speak with these men – and yet how to speak with them and not have them speak with us in a manner that we should not like, that was the main point. It was with a great deal of impatience that we lay still one whole day and saw their boats come on shore and go on board again, and we were so irresolute all the while that we knew not what to do. At last I told my men it was absolutely necessary we should speak with them, and seeing we could not agree upon the method how to do it friendly and fairly, I was resolved to do it by force, and that if they would take my advice, we would place ourselves in ambuscade upon the land somewhere, that we might see them when they were on shore, and the first man that straggled from the rest we would clap in upon and seize him (and three or four of them if we could). As for our boat, we had secured it in a creek three or four miles up the country, where it was secure enough out of their reach or knowledge.

With this resolution we placed ourselves in two gangs – eleven of us in one place, and only three of us in another – and very close we lay. The place we chose for our ambuscade was on the side of a rising ground almost a mile from the watering place, but where we could see them all come towards the shore, and see them if they did but set their foot on shore.

As we understood afterwards, they had the knowledge of our being upon the island but knew not in what part of it, and were therefore very cautious and wary how they went on shore, and came all very well-armed. This gave us a new difficulty, for in the very first excursion that any of them made from the watering-place, there was not less than twenty of them, all well-armed, and they passed by in our sight. But as we were out of their sight, we were all very well pleased with seeing them go by, and being not obliged to meddle with them or show ourselves.

But we had not long lain in this circumstance, but by what occasion we knew not, five of the gentlemen tars were pleased to be willing to go no further with their companions.

And thinking all safe behind them because they had found no disturbance in their going out, came back the same way, straggling without any guard or regard.

I thought now was our time to show ourselves. So taking them as they came by the place where we lay in ambuscade, we placed ourselves just in their way, and as they were entering a little thicket of trees, we appeared and, calling to them in English, told them they were our prisoners: that if they yielded we would use them very well, but if they offered to resist, they should have no quarter. One of them looking behind, as if he would show us a pair of heels, I called to him and told him if he attempted to run for it he was a dead man, unless he could outrun a musket bullet; and that we would soon let him see we had more men in our company; and so giving the signal appointed, our three men, who lay at a distance, showed themselves in the rear.

When they saw this, one of them, who appeared as their leader, but was only the purser's clerk, asked who we were they must yield to, and if we were Christians. I told them, jestingly, we were good honest Christian pirates, and belonged to Captain Avery (not at all letting them know that I was Avery himself), and if they yielded it was enough; we assured them they should have fair quarter and good usage upon our honour, but that they must resolve immediately, or else they would be surrounded with 500 men, and we could not answer for what they might do to them.

They yielded presently upon this news, and delivered their arms, and we carried them away to our tent, which we had built near the place where our boat lay. Here I entered into a particular serious discourse with them about Captain Avery, for it was this I wanted upon several accounts. First, I wanted to enquire what news they had had of us in Europe, and then

67

to give them ideas of our numbers and power as romantic as I could.

They told us that they had heard of the great booty Captain Avery had taken in the Bay of Bengal. And among the rest, a bloody story was related of Avery himself, viz. that he ravished the Great Mogul's daughter (who was going to be married to the Prince of Pegu), that we ravished and forced all the ladies attending her train, and then threw them into the sea or cut their throats, and that we had gotten a booty of ten million in gold and silver, besides an inestimable treasure of jewels, diamonds, pearls, etc. but that we had committed most inhuman barbarities on the innocent people that fell into our hands. They then told us – but in a broken imperfect account – how the Great Mogul had resented it, and that he had raised a great army against the English factories, resolving to root them out of his dominions. But that the company had appeased him by presents, and by assuring him that the men who did it were rebels to the English Government, and that the Queen of England would hang them all whenever they could be taken. I smiled at that and told them Captain Avery would give them leave to hang him and all his men, when they could take them, but that I could assure him they were too strong to be taken, and that if the Government of England went about to provoke them, Captain Avery would soon make those seas too hot for the English, and they might even give over their East India trade, for they little thought of the circumstances Captain Avery was in.

This I did, as well as to know what notions you had of us in England as to give a formidable account of us, and of our circumstances to England, which I knew might be of use to us several ways hereafter. Then I made him tell his part, which he did freely enough. He told us that indeed they had received an account in England that we were exceeding strong; that we had several gangs of pirates from the Spanish West Indies that had taken great booties there, and were gone all to Madagascar to join Captain Avery; that he had taken three great East India ships, one Dutch and two Portuguese, which they had converted into men-of-war; that he had 6,000 men under his command; that he had twelve ships, whereof three carried sixty guns apiece, and six more of them, from forty to fifty guns; that they had built a large fort to secure their habitations; and that they had two large towns, one on one side, one on the other of a river, covered by the said fort, and two great platforms or batteries of guns to defend the entrance where their ships rode; that they had an immense invaluable treasure; and that it was said Captain Avery was resolved to people the whole island of Madagascar with Europeans and to get women from Jamaica and the Leeward Islands, and that it was not doubted but he would subdue, and make himself king of that country, if he was let alone a little longer.

I had enjoined my men, in the first place, not to let him know that I was Avery but that I was one of his captains; and in the next place, not to say a word but just 'Ay', and 'No', as things occurred, and leave the rest to me. I heard him patiently out in all the particulars above, and when he had done, I told him it was true, Captain Avery was in the island of Madagascar, and that several other societies of buccaneers and freebooters were joined him from the Spanish West Indies. 'For,' said I, 'the plenty and ease of our living here is such, and we are so safe from all the world, that we do not doubt but we shall be 20,000 men in a very little time, when two ships which we have sent to the West Indies shall come back, and shall have told the buccaneers at the Bay of Campeche how we live here.

'But,' said I, 'you in England greatly wrong Captain Avery, our General,' (so I called myself, to advance our credit), 'for I can assure you that except plundering the ship and taking that immense booty which he got in the great ship where the Great Mogul's daughter was, there was not the least injury done to the lady, no ravishing or violence to her or any of her attendance. And this,' said I, 'you may take of my certain knowledge, for,' said I, 'I was on board the ship with our General all the while. And if any of the Princess' women were lain with,' said I, 'on board the other ship – as I believe most of them were – yet it was done with their own consent and goodwill, and not otherwise. And they were all dismissed afterwards, without so much as being put in fear or apprehensions of life or honour.'

This I assured him (as indeed it was just) and told him I hoped if ever he came safe to England, he would do Captain Avery and all of us justice in that particular case.

As to our being well fortified on the island, and our numbers, I assured them all they were far from thinking too much of us; that we had a very good fleet, and a very good harbour for them, that we were not afraid of any force from Europe, either by land or water, that it was, indeed, in vain to pretend to attack us by force – that the only way for the Government of England to bring us back to our duty would be to send a proclamation from England with the Queen's pardon for our General and all his people, if they came in by a certain time. 'And,' added I, 'we know you want money in England: I dare say,' said I, 'our General, Captain Avery, and his particular gang who have the main riches, would not grudge to advance five or six million ducats to the government to give them leave to return in peace to England, and sit down quietly with the rest.'

This discourse, I suppose, was the ground of the rumour you have had in England, that Avery has offered to come in and submit, and would give six million for his pardon. For as these men were soon after this dismissed and went back to England, there is no doubt but they gave a particular account of the conference they had with me, who they called one of Captain Avery's captains.

We kept these five men six or seven days, and we pretended to show them the country from some of the hills, calling it our own and pointing every way how many miles we extended ourselves. We made them believe also that all the rest of the country was at our disposal, that the whole island was at our beck. We told them we had treasure enough to enrich the whole kingdom of England, that our General had several million in diamonds, and we had many tons of silver and gold, that we had fifty large barns full of all sorts of goods – as well European as Indian – and that it would be truly the best way for England to do as they said, namely to invite us all home by a proclamation with a pardon. And if they would do this, said I, they can ask no reasonable sum but our General might advance it, besides getting home such a body of stout able seamen as we were, such a number of ships and such a quantity of rich goods.

We had several long discourses with them upon these heads, and our frequent offering this part to them with a kind of feeling warmth (for it was what we all desired) has caused, I doubt not, the rumour of such great offers made by us and of a letter sent by me to the Queen, to beg her Majesty's pardon for myself and my company, and offering ten million of money advance to the Queen for the public service – all of which is a mere fiction of the brain of those which have published it. Neither were we in any condition to make such an offer, neither did I, or any of my crew or company, ever write a letter or petition to the Queen or to anyone in the government, or make any application in the case other than as above, which was only matter of conversation or private discourse.

Nor were we so strong in men or ships, or anything like it. You have heard of the number of ships which we had now with us, which amounted to two ships and a sloop and no more except the prize in which we took the Mogul's daughter (which ship we called, *The Great Mogul*), but she was fit for nothing, for she would neither sail nor steer worth a farthing, and indeed was fit for no use but a hulk, or a guardship.

As to numbers of men, they belied us strangely, and particularly they seemed only to mistake thousands for hundreds. For whereas they told us that you in England had a report of our being 6,000 men, I must acknowledge that I think we were never, when we were at the most, above 600. And at the time when I quitted the country, I left about 108 men there, and no more, and I am assured all the number that now remains there is not above twenty-two men, no, not in the whole island.

Well, we thought however that it was no business of ours at that time to undeceive them in their high opinion of our great strength, so we took care to magnify ourselves, and the strength of our General – meaning myself – that they might carry the story to England, depending upon it *that a tale loses nothing in the carrying*. When they told us of our fort, and the batteries at the mouth of the river where our ships lay, we insinuated that it was a place where we did not fear all the fleets in the world attacking us and, when they told us of the number of men, we strove to make them believe that they were much many more.

At length the poor men began to be tired of us, and indeed we began to be tired of them. For we began to be afraid very much that they would pry a little way into our affairs – and that a little too narrowly that way. So as they began to solicit their deliverance, we began to listen to their importunities. In a word, we agreed to dismiss them, and accordingly we gave them leave to go away to the watering-place as if they had made their escape from us, which they did, carrying away their heads full of those unlikely projected things which you have heard above.

In all this, however, I had not the good luck to advance one step towards my own escape; and here is one thing remarkable, viz. that the great mass of wealth I had gotten together was so far from forwarding my deliverance that it really was the only thing that hindered it most effectually. And I was so sensible of it that I resolved at once to be gone and leave all my wealth behind me, except some jewels, as several of our men had done already. For many of them were so impatient of staying here that they found means to get away, some and some, with no more money than they could carry about them. Particularly, thirteen of our men made themselves a kind of shallop with a mast and sail, and went for the Red Sea, having two pedreros for her defence, and every man 1,000 pieces of eight and no more, except that one MacMow, an Irishman who was their captain, had five rubies and a diamond, which he got among the plunder of the Mogul's ship.

These men, as I heard, got safe to Mecca in the Arabian Gulf, where they fetched the coffee, and their captain managed for them all so well that of pirates he made them merchants, laid out all the stock in coffee and got a vessel to carry it up the Red Sea to Suez, where they sold it to the factors for the European merchants, and came all safe to Alexandria, where they parted the money again. And then everyone separated as they thought fit, and went their own way.

We heard of this by mere accident afterwards, and I confess I envied their success. And though it was a great while after this that I took a like run, yet you may be sure I formed a resolution from that time to do the like. And most of the time that I stayed after this was employed in picking out a suitable gang that I might depend upon – as well to trust with the secret of my going away as to take with me – and on whom I might depend, and they on me, for keeping one another's council when we should come into Europe.

It was in pursuit of this resolution that I went this little voyage to the south of the island, and the gang I took with me proved very trusty, but we found no opportunity then for our escape. Two of the men that we took prisoners would fain have gone with us, but we resolved to trust none of them with the real and true discovery of our circumstances, and as we had made them believe mighty things of ourselves, and of the posture of our settlement – that we had 5,000 men, twelve men-of-war, and the like – we were resolved they should carry the delusion away with them, and that nobody should undeceive them. Because, though we had not such an immense wealth as was reported and so as to be able to offer ten million for our pardon, yet we had a very great treasure. And being nothing near so strong as they had imagined, we might have been made a prey with all our riches to any set of adventurers who might undertake to attempt us by consent of the Government of England, and make the expedition, *no purchase no pay*.

For this reason we civilly declined them, told them we had wealth enough and therefore did not now cruise abroad as we used to do unless we should hear of another wedding of a king's daughter, or unless some rich fleet or some heathen kingdom was to be attempted, and that therefore a newcomer or any body of newcomers, could do themselves no good by coming over to us. If any gang of pirates or buccaneers would go upon their adventures, and when they had made themselves rich would come and settle with us, we would take them into our protection and give them land to build towns and habitations for themselves – and so in time we might become a great nation, and inhabit the whole island. I told them the Romans themselves were, at first, no better than such a gang of rovers as we were, and who knew but our General, Captain Avery, might lay the foundation of as great an empire as they.

These big words amazed the fellows, and answered my end to a tittle; for they told such rodomontading stories of us when they came back to their ships, and from them it spread so universally all over the East Indies (for they were outward bound), that none of the English or Dutch ships would come near Madagascar again if they could help it for a great while, for fear of us. And we, who were soon after this dwindled away to less than 100 men, were very glad to have them think us too strong to meddle with, or so strong that nobody durst come near us.

After these men were gone, we roved about to the east side of the island and, in a word, knew not what to do or what course to take, for we durst not put out to sea in such a bauble of a boat as we had under us, but, tired at last, we came back to the south point of the island again. In our rounding the island we saw a great English-built ship at sea, but at too far distance to speak with her, and if it had not, we knew not what to have said to her, for we were not strong enough to attack her. We judged, by her course, she stood away from the Isle of St Maurice or Mauritius, for the Cape of Good Hope, and must as we supposed have come from the Malabar coast, bound home for England – so we let her go.

We are now returned back to our settlement on the north part of the island; and I have singled out about twelve or thirteen bold brave fellows, with whom I have resolved to venture to the Gulf of Persia. Twenty more of our men have agreed to carry us thither as passengers in the sloop and try their own fortunes afterwards, for they allow we are enough to go together. We resolve, when we come to Bassora, to separate into three companies, as if we did not know one another; to dress ourselves as merchants – for now we look like hell-hounds and vagabonds, but when we are well-dressed, we expect to look as other men do. If I come thither, I purpose, with two more, to give my companions the slip and travel as Armenians through Persia to the Caspian Sea, and so to Constantinople. And I doubt not we shall, one way or other, find our way with our merchandise and money to come into France, if not quite home to my own country. Assure yourself, when I arrive in any part of Christendom I will give you a further account of my adventures.

Your friend and servant,

AVERY

A SECOND LETTER

Sir,

I wrote my last letter to you from Madagascar, where I continued so long till my people began to drop from me, some and some, and indeed I had at last but few left, so that I began to apprehend they would give an account in Europe how weak I was and how easy it was to attack me. Nay, and to make their peace, might some of them at least offer their service to be pilots to my port, and might guide the fleets or ships that should attempt me.

With these apprehensions, I not only was uneasy myself but made all my men uneasy too. For, as I was resolved to attempt my own escape, I did not care how many of my men went before me. But this you must take with you by the by, that I never let them imagine that I intended to stir from the spot myself (I mean, after my return from the ramble that I had taken round the island, of which I have given you an account), but that I resolved to take up my rest in Madagascar as long as I lived. Indeed, before I said otherwise, as I wrote you before, and made them all promise to fetch me away, but now I gave it out that I was resolved to live and die here. And therefore, a little before I resolved upon going, I set to work to build me a new house and to plant me a pretty garden at a distance from our fort. Only I had a select company to whom I communicated everything, and who resolved that, at last, we would go all together, but that we would do it our own way.

When I had finished my new house (and a mighty palace you would say it was, if you had been to see it), I removed to it, with eight of the gang that were to be my fellow adventurers. And to this place we carried all our private wealth, that is to say, jewels and gold – as to our share of silver, as it was too heavy to remove, and must be done in public, I was obliged to leave it behind. But we had a stratagem for that too, and it was thus.

We had a sloop as you have heard, and she lay in our harbour, it is true. But she lay ready to sail upon any occasion. And the men who were of our confederacy, who were not with me at my country house, were twelve in number. These men made a proposal that they would take the sloop and go away to the coast of Malabar, or where else they could speed to their mind and buy a freight of rice for the public account. In a free state as we were, everybody was free to go wherever they would, so that nobody opposed them, the only dispute at any time was about taking the vessel we had to go in. However, as these men seemed only to act upon the public account and to go to buy provisions, nobody offered to deny them the sloop, so they prepared for their voyage. Just as they were ready to go, one of them starts it to the rest that it was very hazardous and difficult to run such a length every now and then to get a little rice, and if they would go, why should they not bring a good quantity? This was soon resolved. So they agreed they should take money with them to buy a good ship wherever they could find her, and then to buy a loading of rice to fill her up, and so come away with her.

When this was agreed, they resolved to take no money out of the grand stock, but to take such men's money as were gone and had left their money behind, and this being consented to truly, my friends took the occasion and took all their own money, and mine (being sixty-four little chests of pieces of eight), and carried it on board, as if it had been of men that were pricked-run[19], and nobody took any notice of it. These twelve men had also now got twelve more with them – under pretence of manning a ship, if we should buy one – and, in this pickle, away they put to sea.

We had due notice of everything that was done, and having a signal given of the time they resolved to go, we packed up all our treasure and began our march to the place appointed, which from our quarters was about forty miles further north.

Our habitation, that is to say my new house, was about sixteen miles up the country, so that the rest of our people could have no notice of our march, neither did they miss us, at least, as I heard of, for we never heard any more of them. Nor can I imagine what condition or circumstance they can be in at present if they are still upon the place as, however, I believe some of them are.

We joined our comrades, with a great deal of ease, about three days afterwards, for we marched but softly, and they lay by for us. The night before we went on board, we made them a signal by fire, as we had appointed, to let them know where we were and that we were at hand, so they sent their boat and fetched us off, and we embarked without any notice taken by the rest.

As we were now loose and at sea, our next business was to resolve whither we should go and I soon governed the point, resolving for Bassora in the Gulf of Persia, where I knew we might shift for ourselves. Accordingly, we steered away for the Arabian coast, and had good weather for some time, even till we made the land at a great distance, when we steered eastward along the shore.

We saw several ships in our way, bound to and from the Red Sea, as we supposed, and at another time we would have been sure to have spoken with them. But we had done pirating. Our business now was how to get off, and make our way to some retreat, where we might enjoy what we had got. So we took no notice of anything by the way, but, when we were thus sailing merrily along, the weather began to change, the evening grew black and cloudy, and threatened a storm. We were in sight of a little island (I know nothing of its name), under which we might have anchored with safety enough, but our people made light of it and went on.

About an hour after sunset the wind began to rise, and blew hard at N.E. and at N.E. by N. and in two hours' time increased to such a tempest as in all my rambles I never met with the like. We were not able to carry a knot of sail, or to know what to do but to stow everything close and let her drive, and in this condition we continued all the night, all the next day, and part of the night after. Towards morning the storm abated a little, but not so as to give us any prospect of pursuing our voyage. All the ease we had was that we could just carry a little sail to steady the vessel, and run away before it, which we did at that violent rate, that we never abated till we made land on the east side of Madagascar – the very land we came from, only on the other side of the island.

However, we were glad we had any place to run to for harbour, so we put in under the lee of a point of land that gave us shelter from the wind, and where we came to an anchor after being all of us almost dead with the fatigue. And if our sloop had not been an extraordinary sea-boat, she could never have borne such a sea for twelve days together as we were in, the worst I ever saw before or since. We lay here to refresh ourselves about twenty days, and, indeed, the wind blew so hard all the while that, if we had been disposed to go to sea, we could not have done it. And, being here, about seven of our men began to repent their bargain and left us, which I was not sorry for. It seems the principal reason of their looking back was their being of those who had left their money behind them. They did not leave us without our consent and therefore our carpenters built them a boat during the three weeks we stayed here, and fitted it very handsomely for them, with a cabin for their convenience and a mast and sail, with which they might very well sail round to our settlement, as we suppose they did. We gave them firearms and ammunition sufficient, and left them furnishing themselves with provisions. And this we suppose was the boat (though with other men in it) which adventured afterwards as far as the Cape of Good Hope and was taken up by a Portuguese in distress, by which means they got passage for themselves to Lisbon, pretending they had made their escape from the pirates at Madagascar. But we were told that the Portuguese captain took a great deal of their money from them, under pretence of keeping it from his own seamen, and that when they came on shore and began to claim it, he threatened them with taking them up, and prosecuting them for pirates, which made them compound with him, and take about 10,000 dollars for above 120,000 which they had with them, which, by the way, was but a scurvy trick. They had, it seems, a considerable quantity of gold among them, which they had the wit to conceal from the captain of the ship, and which was enough for such fellows as them, and more than they well knew what to do with. So that they were rich enough still – though the Portugal captain was nevertheless a knave for all that.

We left them here as I have said, and put to sea again, and, in about twenty days' sail, having pretty good weather, we arrived at the Gulf of Persia. It would be too long to give you an account of the particular fortunes of some of our people after this, the variety of which would fill a volume by itself. But in the first place, we, who were determined to travel, went on shore at Bassora, leaving the rest of our men to buy rice and load the larger vessel back to their comrades, which they promised to do, but how far they performed I know not.

We were thirteen of us that went on shore here, from whence we hired a kind of barge, or rather a bark, which, after much difficulty, and very unhandy doings of the men who we had hired, brought us to Babylon, or Baghdad, as it is now called.

Our treasure was so great that, if it had been known what we had about us, I am of opinion we should never have troubled Europe with our company. However, we got safe to Babylon or Baghdad, where we kept ourselves incognito for a while, took a house by ourselves, and lay four or five days still, till we had got vests and long gowns made to appear abroad in as Armenian merchants. After we had got clothes and looked like other people, we began to appear abroad, and I, that from the beginning had meditated my escape by myself, began now to put it into practice. And walking one morning upon the bank of the River Euphrates, I mused with myself what course I should take to make off, and get quite away from the gang and let them not so much as suspect me.

While I was walking here, comes up one of my comrades and one who I always took for my particular friend. 'I know what you are employed in,' said he, 'while you seem only to be musing and refreshing yourself with the cool breeze.' 'Why,' said I, 'what am I musing about?' 'Why,' said he, 'you are studying how you should get away from us, but, muse upon it as long as you will,' says he, 'you shall never go without me, for I am resolved to go with you which way soever you take.' 'It is true,' says I, 'I was musing about which way I should go without you, for though I would be willing to part company, yet you cannot think I would go alone. And you know I have chosen you out from all the company to be the partner of all my adventures.'

'Very well,' says he, 'but I am to tell you now that it is not only necessary that we should not go all together, but our men have all concluded that we should make our escape every one for himself, and should separate as we could, so that you need make no secret of your design any more than of the way you intend to take.'

I was glad enough of this news, and it made me very easy in the preparations we made for our setting out. And the first thing we did was to get us more clothes, having some made of one fashion, some of another. But my friend and I – who resolved to keep together – made us clothes after the fashion of the Armenian merchants, whose country we pretended to travel through.

In the meantime, five of our men dressed like merchants, and laying out their money in raw silk and wrought silks, and other goods of the country proper for Europe (in which they were directed by an English merchant there), resolved to take the usual route and travel by the caravans from Babylon to Aleppo, and so to Skenderun[20], and we stayed and saw them and their bales go off in boats for a great town on the Euphrates, where the caravans begin to take up the passengers. The other six divided themselves, one half of them went for Agra (the country of the Great Mogul), resolving to go down the River Hooghly to Bengal, but whither they went afterward or what course they took, I never knew, neither whether they really went at all or not.

The other three went by sea in a Persian vessel back from the Red Sea to the Gulf of Mocha, and I heard of them all three at Marseilles, but whither they went afterwards I never knew, nor could I come to speak with them even there.

As for me and my friend, we first laid out all the silver we had in European ware such as we knew would vend at

Isfahan, which we carried upon twelve camels, and hiring some servants, as well for our guide as our guard, we set out.

The servants we hired were a kind of Arab, but rather looking like the Great Mogul's people than real Arabians. And, when we came into Persia, we found they were looked upon as no better than dogs and were not only used ill but that we were used ill for their sakes, and after we were come three days into the Persian dominions, we found ourselves obliged to part with them. So we gave them three dollars a man to go back again.

They understood their business very well, and knew well enough what was the reason of it, though we did not. However, we found we had committed a great mistake in it, for we perceived that they were so exasperated at being turned off that they vowed to be revenged, and indeed they had their revenge to the full. For the same day, at night, they returned in the dark and set eleven houses on fire in the town where we quartered, which, by the way, had gone near to have cost me my life, and would certainly have done so if in the hurry I had not seized one the incendiaries and delivered him up to them.

The people were so provoked at him that was taken that they fell upon him with all possible fury, as the common incendiary and burner of the town – and presently quitted us, for they had before vowed our destruction, but, as I said, quitted us immediately – and thronged about the wretch they had taken. And, indeed, I made no question but that they would have immediately murdered him, nay, that they would have torn him in pieces before they parted with him. But after they had vented their rage at him for some time with all possible reproaches and indignities, they carried him before the cadi, or judge of the place. The cadi, a wise grave man, answered no: he would not judge him at that time, for they

84

were too hot and passionate to do justice, but they should come with him in the morning when they were cool, and he would hear them.

It is true, this was a most excellent step of the cadi, as to the right way of doing justice. But it did not prove the most expedient in the present occasion, though that was none of his fault neither, for in the night the fellow got out of their hands, by what means or by whose assistance I never heard to this day. And the cadi fined the town a considerable sum for letting a man accused of a capital crime make his escape before he was adjudged, and, as we call it, discharged according to law.

This was an eminent instance of the justice of these people. And though they were doubly enraged at the escape of the fellow, who without doubt was guilty, yet they never opened their mouths against the cadi, but acquiesced in his judgement as in that of an oracle, and submitted to the national censure – or censure according to the custom of their nation – which he had passed upon them in their public capacity for the escape of the man.

We were willing to get out of this place as soon as we could; but we found the people's rage, which wanted an object to vent itself upon, began to threaten us again. So having packed up our goods, and gotten five ordinary camel drivers for our servants in the country, we set out again.

The roads in Persia are not so much frequented as to be well accommodated with inns, so that several times we were obliged to lodge upon the ground in the way. But our new servants took care to furnish us with lodging, for as soon as we let them know we wanted rest and inclined to stop, they set up a tent for us in so short a time that we were scarce able to imagine it possible, and under this we encamped, our camels being just by us, and our servants and bales lying all hard by.

Once or twice we lodged in public inns, built at the King of Persia's charge. These are fair large buildings, built square, like a large inn, they have all of them large stables and good forage for the camels and horses, and apartments for perhaps two or three hundred people, and they are called caravanserais, as being built to entertain whole caravans of travellers. On the great roads to Tauris and the side of Turkey they are all fortified, and are able to entertain five or six thousand people, and have a stock to furnish what number of men can come with provisions. Nay, it has been known that whole armies of the Persians have on their march been furnished with provisions in one of these caravanserais, and that they have killed 2,000 sheep for them in one night's time.

In this manner we travelled to Isfahan, the capital of Persia, where appearing as merchants, and with several camels laden with merchandise, we passed all possibility of suspicion, and being perfectly easy we continued here some time, sold our cargoes, and would gladly have remitted the money to other places, as for Constantinople in particular. But we found the Turks and Persians have no such thing as an exchange by bills running between them and other nations – no, nor between one town and another.

We were invited here by a sudden accident to have gone home by the Caspian Sea and Astrakhan – so through Muscovy. But I had heard so much of the barbarity of the Russians, the dangerous navigation of the Caspian Sea by reason of the calms and shoals, the hazard of being robbed by the Tartars on the River Volga, and the like, that I chose to travel to Constantinople, a journey through deserts, over mountains and wastes, among so many sorts of barbarians that I would run any kind of hazards by sea before I would attempt such a thing again.

It would deserve another history to let you into all the different circumstances of this journey, how well I was used by some, and how ill by others. Nay, how well by some Mahometans, how ill by some Christians. But it shall suffice to tell you that I am at present at Constantinople. And, though I write this here, I do not purpose to send it to you till I come to Marseilles in France, from whence I intend to go in some inland town, where, as they have perhaps no notion of the sea, so they will not be inquisitive after us.

I am, etc.

NOTES

1. Campeche is a port, city, and state of Mexico, and 'Campeche wood' was another name for logwood.
2. Puno is a city in Peru.
3. The Isthmus of Darien, today known as Panama, is the narrow strip of land linking North and South America.
4. A sugar-mill or sugar works, although here used more broadly perhaps to mean an outlet for provisions.
5. St Domingo here refers to the Dominican Republic, which was formerly known as Santo Domingo (now the name of its capital city).
6. St Christopher Island in the West Indies, also known as St Kitts-Nevis, or, officially, the Federation of St Christopher and Nevis.
7. Pernambuco, now Recife, is a port in Brazil.
8. A pedrero is a weapon for discharging stones, broken iron, partridge-shot, and for firing salutes.
9. Guayaquil is today the name of the city located on the Guayas river, in Ecuador.
10. The date here is erroneous. Having been on their voyage a year and seven days, they would reach St Julien on 27th November.
11. Again the date is erroneous, the ship having doubled the Cape on 13th March and arrived in Madagascar on 7th April.
12. In fact, St Augustine's Bay in Madagascar.
13. Unanimously, or without objection.
14. Another erroneous date – this should be a year earlier, 1693.
15. The Coromandel Coast, south-east India.
16. A large rope or small cable used for mooring or anchoring.
17. Pegu (Bago) is a city and district in Myanmar, Burma.
18. Bassora is now Basra in Iraq.
19. 'Pricked-run' here seems to mean marked off.
20. Iskenderun is a port in Turkey.

BIOGRAPHICAL NOTE

Born in London in 1661, the son of a butcher and tallow chandler, Daniel Defoe is widely considered the first English novelist. Educated at a dissenting school and intended for the Presbyterian Church, Defoe instead embarked on a career in trade, travelling to France, Spain, and Holland as a hosiery merchant and tile manufacturer. This venture ended in bankruptcy in 1691, by which time he had already begun writing political tracts. He worked as an agent for William III, and his myriad pamphlets, tracts and works of journalism indicate his capacity to elaborate satirically or otherwise the full spectrum of political and social perspectives. Defoe was in fact imprisoned in 1703 for a tract that attacked Dissenters. He was then employed by the Tory politician, Robert Harley, as a secret agent to gauge public opinion, and concurrently wrote a thrice-weekly newspaper called *The Review* almost single-handedly. Contentious pamphlets led to a second prison sentence in 1713, and only political manoeuvres enabled him to escape a sentence for libel in 1715.

In 1719, the seemingly autobiographical novel, *Robinson Crusoe*, appeared: a book that has influenced generations of readers, authors such as Jules Verne, Robert Louis Stevenson, and J.M. Coetzee, and many film-makers. Further works of fiction followed, including *Moll Flanders* (1722), *Journal of the Plague Year* (1722), and *Roxana* (1724), all purportedly first-hand accounts of extraordinary lives. These powerful narratives in plain prose are the most famous works by a prolific writer whose vast and varied output encompassed history, biography, crime and travel writing. Defoe died in 1731, his contribution to the evolution of the English novel one aspect only of his extraordinary literary legacy.

HESPERUS PRESS – 100 PAGES

Hesperus Press, as suggested by the Latin motto, is committed to bringing near what is far – far both in space and time. Works written by the greatest authors, and unjustly neglected or simply little known in the English-speaking world, are made accessible through new translations and a completely fresh editorial approach. Through these short classic works, each little more than 100 pages in length, the reader will be introduced to the greatest writers from all times and all cultures.

For more information on Hesperus Press, please visit our website: **www.hesperuspress.com**

To place an order, please contact:
Grantham Book Services
Isaac Newton Way
Alma Park Industrial Estate
Grantham
Lincolnshire NG31 9SD
Tel: +44 (0) 1476 541080
Fax: +44 (0) 1476 541061
Email: orders@gbs.tbs-ltd.co.uk

SELECTED TITLES FROM HESPERUS PRESS

Gustave Flaubert *Memoirs of a Madman*
Alexander Pope *Scriblerus*
Ugo Foscolo *Last Letters of Jacopo Ortis*
Anton Chekhov *The Story of a Nobody*
Joseph von Eichendorff *Life of a Good-for-nothing*
Mark Twain *The Diary of Adam and Eve*
Giovanni Boccaccio *Life of Dante*
Victor Hugo *The Last Day of a Condemned Man*
Joseph Conrad *Heart of Darkness*
Edgar Allan Poe *Eureka*
Emile Zola *For a Night of Love*
Giacomo Leopardi *Thoughts*
Nikolai Gogol *The Squabble*
Franz Kafka *Metamorphosis*
Herman Melville *The Enchanted Isles*
Leonardo da Vinci *Prophecies*
Charles Baudelaire *On Wine and Hashish*
William Makepeace Thackeray *Rebecca and Rowena*
Wilkie Collins *Who Killed Zebedee?*
Théophile Gautier *The Jinx*
Charles Dickens *The Haunted House*
Luigi Pirandello *Loveless Love*
Fyodor Dostoevsky *Poor People*
E.T.A. Hoffmann *Mademoiselle de Scudéri*
Henry James *In the Cage*
Francesco Petrarch *My Secret Book*
D.H. Lawrence *The Fox*
Percy Bysshe Shelley *Zastrozzi*